THE
SNAKE-
CATCHER'S
DAUGHTER

Michael Pearce was raised in Anglo-Egyptian Sudan, where his fascination for language began. He later trained as a Russian interpreter but moved away from languages to follow an academic career, first as a lecturer in English and the History of Ideas, and then as an administrator. Michael Pearce now lives in London and is best known as the author of the award-winning *Mamur Zapt* books.

ALSO BY MICHAEL PEARCE

The Mamur Zapt Series

The Dmitri Kameron Series

The Seymour of Special Branch Series

MICHAEL PEARCE

THE
SNAKE-CATCHER'S DAUGHTER

HarperCollins*Publishers*

HarperCollins*Publishers* Ltd
1 London Bridge Street,
London SE1 9GF

www.harpercollins.co.uk

First published in Great Britain by
HarperCollins*Publishers* 1994

This paperback edition 2017
1

A catalogue record for this book is
available from the British Library

ISBN: 978-0-00-825943-3

Printed and bound in the UK

MIX
Paper from
responsible sources

FSC
www.fsc.org
FSC™ C007454

FSC is a non-profit international organisation established
to promote the responsible management of the world's forests.
Products carrying the FSC label are independently certified
to assure consumers that they come from forests that are managed
to meet the social, economic and ecological needs
of present and future generations.

Find out more about HarperCollins and the environment at
www.harpercollins.co.uk/green

1

One evening when Owen got home he found a girl in his bed.

'Hello!' he said. 'What's this?'

'I'm a present,' she said.

'Who from?'

'We can go into details later.'

'A member of the British Administration is not allowed to accept presents,' he said, stuffily.

And not altogether honestly. For the Mamur Zapt, Head of Cairo's Secret Police, was not, strictly speaking, a member of the British Administration but a member of the Egyptian Administration; and whereas the British, under Cromer's strait-laced regime had not been allowed to accept bribes, the Khedive's servants had always taken a more relaxed view.

'All the world knows about your Zeinab,' said the girl, pouting.

Owen rather hoped that all the world did *not* know about Zeinab and was more than a little surprised that the girl did.

'Ah, yes, but she is not a present.'

'I don't need to stay a present,' said the girl.

'Off you go!'

'Like this?' demanded the girl, pulling the sheet back. Underneath she was completely naked.

'If that's the way you came.'

The girl, rather sulkily, rose from the bed and picked up a dress that was lying across a chair. A European dress, but was she European? Such questions were on the whole unprofitable in cosmopolitan Cairo. A Levantine, say, and a beautiful one.

Owen began to wonder if perhaps he should make more of an effort to get to the bottom of this attempt to bribe him. Bottom, as a matter of fact, was exactly what he was contemplating just at this moment . . .

'Oh yes?' said Zeinab belligerently when he told her.

'Oh yes?' said Garvin, the Commandant of the Cairo Police Force, sceptically.

'Oh yes?' said everyone in the bar when he happened to mention it. 'What happened next?'

'She put on her veil and left,' said Owen with a firmness which did not altogether, unfortunately, dampen speculation.

'Leaving her honour behind her?' suggested someone.

'I wouldn't have thought so.'

Leaving behind her, actually, a small embroidered amulet, the sort of thing you could pick up in one of the bazaars. Inside it was a single quite respectably sized diamond. Perfume stayed on his fingers long after the girl was gone.

'So that is why you told everybody,' said his friend, Paul. Paul was ADC to the Consul-General and wise in the ways of the world; wise, at any rate, in the ways of protecting your back.

Owen nodded.

'People must always be attempting to bribe you,' observed Paul.

'Not so much now,' said Owen. 'When I first came, certainly.'

He had been in post for nearly three years.

'And it has taken them all that time to find out?' said Paul, marvelling.

'That I couldn't be bribed?'

'That you weren't worth bribing.'

'Someone,' Owen pointed out, hurt, 'has apparently still not found out.'

'Yes,' said Paul. 'Odd, isn't it?'

The next morning one of the orderlies came in in great agitation.

'Effendi,' he said, 'the Bimbashi's donkey is not here.'

Owen laid down his pen.

'Someone's stolen it?'

'No, no. It has not been here all morning. The Bimbashi has not come in.'

This was unusual. McPhee, the Deputy Commandant, always came in.

'A touch of malaria, perhaps,' said Owen, picking up his pen again. 'Send someone to find out.'

A buzz of excited chatter outside his door told him when the someone returned.

'Well?'

'Effendi,' said the orderly, with a long face, 'the Bimbashi's not there.'

'He has not been there all night,' put in another of the orderlies.

'Hm!' What members of the Administration did in the night was their business and it was normally wisest not to inquire. McPhee, however, was not like that. He was very puritanical; some would say undeveloped. He was the sort of man who if he had been in England would have joined that strange new organization, the Boy Scouts. After some consideration, Owen went in to see Garvin.

Garvin, also, took it seriously.

'He'd have let us know if it was work, wouldn't he?'

'It can hardly be play,' said Owen.

'He won't be sleeping it off, certainly,' said Garvin. Owen thought that the remark was possibly directed at him.

'What I meant was, that he's not one to let his private life interfere with his work,' he said, and then realized that sounded unnecessarily priggish. Garvin tended to have that effect on people.

'What was he doing yesterday?' asked Garvin. 'Was it something he was likely to get knocked over the head doing?'

Apparently not. The office had been quiet all day. Indeed, it had been quiet all week. The weather, hot always, of course, had been exceptionally so for the last fortnight, which had brought almost all activity in Cairo, including crime, to a standstill.

'You'd better get people out looking for him,' said Garvin.

Owen didn't like Garvin treating him as just another deputy. The Mamur Zapt reported – in form, of course – to the Khedive and it was only for convenience that Owen was lodged in the police headquarters at Bab-el-Khalk. However, he quite liked McPhee and wasn't going to quibble.

Garvin, in fact, was genuinely concerned and wasn't doing this just as an administrative power game.

'Get them all out,' he said. 'They've got nothing better to do.'

It was now nearly noon and the sun was at its hottest, and this was therefore not the view of the ordinary police-man. If turned out now they would probably make for the nearest patch of shade.

Besides, what were they to look for? A body? There were thousands of places in Cairo where bodies might be lying and usually it was simplest to allow them to declare their presence later – in the heat it would not be much later – by their smell. There was, however, an easier solution.

'You all know the Bimbashi's donkey,' said Owen. 'Find it.'

'Look for a donkey?' expostulated Nikos, his Official Clerk. 'You can't have the whole Police Force out looking for a donkey!'

'Why not?'

'It sounds bad. Have you thought how it would look in the pages of *Al-Lewa*?'

Owen had not. He could just imagine, though, what the Nationalist press would make of it. The newspapers would be full of it for weeks. He stuck doggedly, however, to his guns. Nikos changed tack.

'How much are you offering for information?' he asked practically.

'It's McPhee, after all.'

'Five pounds?'

'Good God, no!' said Owen, shocked. 'We'd have the whole city bringing us donkeys if we offered that. One pound Egyptian.'

'I thought, as it was an Englishman –' suggested Nikos.

'One-fifty.'

'And in the police –'

'Two pounds,' said Owen. 'We'll make it two pounds. That is my limit.'

'It ought to be enough,' said Nikos, who believed in value for money.

Word went out to the bazaars by methods which only Nikos knew and Owen sat down to await results. They came by nightfall.

'What the hell is this?' said Garvin.

Owen explained.

'It's like a bloody donkey market,' said Garvin.

Owen went down into the courtyard to sort things out. Nikos watched with interest. Believing that decisions should be taken where knowledge lay, which certainly wasn't at the top, Owen enlisted the aid of the orderlies, whom he stationed at the entrance to the courtyard.

'You know the Bimbashi's donkey,' he said. 'All the others are to be turned away.'

Within an hour the usual torpor of the Bab-el-Khalk was restored.

By now it was dark.

'You stay here,' he ordered.

The orderlies, appeased by the prospect of a few extra piastres and full of self-importance at their newly-significant role, were quite content to stay on. Meanwhile, Owen went down to the club for a drink.

'I gather there's some problem about McPhee,' said a man at his elbow.

'Maybe,' said Owen, non-committally.

'Not been knocked on the head, has he? I wouldn't want that to happen. He's a funny bloke, not everyone's cup of tea, but I quite like him.'

'I dare say he's all right.'

His neighbour looked at him.

'Like that, is it?'

Owen gave a neutral smile.

'You're not saying? Fair enough. Only I hope he's all right.'

Owen, who had previously regarded the eccentric McPhee as much with irritation as with affection, was surprised to find that he felt rather the same.

'What's happened to the drink this evening?' he asked. 'It's bloody lukewarm.'

'It's the heat,' someone said. 'Even the ice is melting.'

Owen decided to go back to the Bab-el-Khalk. He put down his glass and headed for the door, spurred on by hearing someone say, 'Sorry I'm late, old man. Couldn't get here for the donkeys.'

There were, indeed, a lot of donkeys outside the Bab-el-Khalk. Since they were refused entry into the courtyard, they congregated in the square in front of the building, blocking the road. Garvin was just leaving the building as he arrived.

'I hope you know what you're doing,' he said.

Unaccountably, there were about half a dozen donkeys inside the courtyard.

'What are they doing here?'

The orderlies looked embarrassed.

'We thought they might be the Bimbashi's donkey,' they said.

'You know damned well they're not!'

'It's not always possible to tell in the dark,' muttered someone.

'We brought them in so that we could see them better.'

Owen knew exactly why they had been brought in. Their enterprising owners, eager for the reward, had slipped the orderlies a few piastres.

'Get them out of here!'

He heard the arguments beginning as he turned into the building.

Nevertheless, it worked. The following morning it was reported that the Bimbashi's donkey had been seen grazing unattended on the edge of the Place of Tombs. The informant had not actually brought the donkey – which told in his favour – but was confident that it was the Bimbashi's donkey. He had seen the Bimbashi on it many times and, yes, indeed – astonishment that anyone could suppose otherwise – he did know one donkey from another. Owen decided to go himself.

'Why don't you send Georgiades?' suggested Nikos, less confident than Owen that this was not a wild goose chase.

'Because he's probably still in bed.'

'He spends too much time in bed if you ask me,' said Nikos. 'Especially since he married that Rosa girl,' he shot after Owen's departing back.

Owen gave a passing wonder to Nikos's own sexual habits. He had always assumed that Nikos cohabited with a filing cabinet, but there had seemed some edge to that remark.

He picked up the informant, one Ibrahim, in the Gamaliya and went with him to the place where he had seen the donkey. It was among the mountainous rubbish heaps which divided the Gamaliya district from the tombs of the Khalifs. The tombs were like houses and some of the rubbish came from their collapse. The rest came from houses in the Gamaliya. This part of the Gamaliya was full of decaying old mansions. From time to time, especially when it rained heavily, a mud-brick wall would dissolve and collapse, leaving a heap of rubble. The area was like a gigantic abandoned building site. Coarse grass grew on some of the heaps of rubble and it was here, contentedly cropping, that they found the donkey.

Even Owen, who was not particularly observant, especially of donkeys, could see at once that it was McPhee's little white animal. He went up to it and examined it. That was certainly McPhee's saddle. It was one of those on which – if you had a good sense of balance – you could sit cross-legged. Apart from that he could see nothing special; no bloodstains, for example.

He made a swift cast round and then, finding nothing, sent back to the Bab-el-Khalk for more men. If McPhee were here, he would be lying among or under the rubble and they would have to search the area systematically.

Ibrahim himself knew little. He passed through the area every day on his way to work and the previous morning had noticed the donkey. Although a worker in the city now, he had, like very many others, come originally from the country and distinguished between donkeys as later generations might distinguish between cars. He had seen at once that it was the Bimbashi's donkey but had not felt it incumbent on him to do anything about it until word had reached him about the reward. He had seen nothing untoward, nothing, indeed, that he could remember about the morning apart from the donkey. He did, however, say that it was not a place where one lingered.

'Why is that, Ibrahim?' asked Owen sympathetically. 'Are there bad men around?'

Ibrahim hesitated.

'Not bad men, effendi –'

He looked over his shoulder as if he was afraid of being overheard.

'Yes?'

'Bad women,' he muttered, and could not be persuaded to say another word.

*   *   *

12

The search went on all morning. By noon, heat spirals were dancing on top of the heaps of masonry and individual slabs of stone were too hot to lift. He gave the men a break in the shade. He hadn't quite abandoned hope of finding McPhee alive, he didn't let himself think about it too much, but he was growing more and more worried. As usual on such occasions a considerable crowd had gathered and he took the opportunity of the break to go among them making inquiries. He also sent some men around the neighbouring houses. None of it produced anything.

He put the men back to work. By about half past three they had covered an area a quarter of a mile wide on either side of the donkey and found nothing. How much wider was it sensible to go?

He made up his mind. It was a long shot – in fact, bearing in mind McPhee's prim, if not downright maidenly nature, it was so long it was almost out of sight, but he had to try anything, and Ibrahim had said –   '

'Selim!' he called.

One of the constables came across, glad to escape for a moment from the relentless searching among the rubble.

'Effendi?'

'Go into the Gamaliya, not far, around here will do, and ask for the local bad women.'

'Ask for the local bad women?' said the constable, stunned.

'That's right,' snapped Owen. 'And when you have found them, come back and tell me.'

The constable pulled himself together.

'Right, effendi,' he said. 'Certainly, effendi. At once!'

He hurried off.

'Some men have all the luck,' said one of the other constables.

'Get on with it!' barked Owen crossly.

Selim took a long time, unsurprisingly; so long, in fact, that Owen went to look for him. He met him just as he was emerging from the Gamaliya. He seemed, however, rather disappointed.

'Effendi,' he said, 'this is not much of a place. Why don't you come with me to the Ezbekiya –'

'Have you found the place?'

'Well, yes, but –'

'OK. Just take me there.'

'What's this?' he heard one constable say to another as they left. 'A threesome?'

Behind an onion stall, in a small, dark, dirty street, a door opened into a room below ground level. In the darkness Owen could just make out a woman on a bed.

'Ya Fatima!' called the constable.

The woman rose from the bed, with difficulty, and waddled across to the door. She was hugely, grotesquely fat and her hands, feet and face were heavily dyed with henna. Her hair was greased with something rancid which he could smell even from outside the door. Eccentric though McPhee was –

'Would the Effendi like to come in?'

'This will do.'

'It would be better if you came in, effendi.'

The constable watched, grinning.

'This is the police,' said Owen sternly, eager for once to assert his status.

The woman's smile vanished.

'Again?' she said angrily. 'They had me over there on Monday!'

'This is a different matter,' he said hastily. 'I want to know the men you were with last night and the night before.'

'Ali, Abdul, Ahmed –'

The list went on.

'No Effendis?'

'No Effendi,' she said coyly. 'Not yet.'

All right, it had been a mistake. McPhee probably didn't know what a brothel was. But what, then, had Ibrahim meant by 'bad women'? And why was this a place where one didn't linger? Why had McPhee come here in the first place? And where was the poor devil now?

That question, at least, was soon answered. Urgent shouts came from the Gamaliya and people came running to fetch him. They led him into a little street not far from the bad woman's and then up a tiny alleyway into what looked like a carpenter's yard. Planks were propped against the walls and on the ground were some unfinished fretted woodwork screens for the meshrebiya windows characteristic of old Cairo. He was dragged across the yard to what looked like an old-fashioned stone cistern with sides about five feet high. A mass of people were gathered around it, all peering down into its inside. Someone was pulled aside and Owen pushed through. He clung to the edge of the cistern and looked down. McPhee was lying at the bottom. Something else, too. The cistern was full of snakes.

Owen shouted for his constables. They came, big men, forcing their way through the crowd.

'Get them out of the way!' said Owen. 'Clear a space.'

The constables linked arms, bowed down and charged the crowd with their heads. They were used to this kind of situation. The smallest accident draws a crowd in Cairo, all sympathetic, all involved and all in the way.

A couple of constables stayed out of the cordon, drew their truncheons and slapped any encroachment of hand, foot or head.

Owen levered himself up on to the edge of the cistern and put his head down into its depths.

'Effendi!' said an anxious voice. It was Selim, who, previously singled out for glory, had suddenly grown in stature and now took upon himself a senior role.

'Get hold of me!'

He felt Selim's grasp tighten and swung himself lower.

The snakes did not move. One or two were lying on McPhee's chest, others coiled beneath his armpits. They all seemed asleep at the moment, perhaps they were digesting a meal, but if he tried to move McPhee he was bound to waken them.

'Effendi,' said Selim, 'is this not something better left to experts?'

A voice at the back of the crowd shouted: 'Abu! Fetch Abu!'

'Pull me up!'

He came back up over the side and lowered his feet to the ground.

'I've got to get him out,' he said. 'Now listen carefully. Two of you, no three, it will be a heavy weight, catch hold of me. I'm going to reach down and get hold of McPhee. I'll try and get a good grip –'

'They'll bite you in the face, effendi!'

Owen swallowed.

'I'm going to do it quickly,' he said. 'Very quickly. As soon as I shout, pull me up. I'll be heavy because I'll be holding McPhee. But you just bloody pull, as fast as you can. The rest of you can help. And Selim!'

'Yes, effendi?'

'There'll be snakes on him. Maybe on me, too. Now, what I want you to do is to catch hold of them –'

'Catch hold?' said Selim faintly.

'And throw them back.'

'Look, effendi,' began Selim, less sure now about the glory.

'Do it quickly and you'll be all right.'

'Effendi –'

'I'm relying on you.'

Selim swallowed.

'Effendi,' he said heroically, 'I will do it.'

'Good man. Remember, speed is the thing.'

'Effendi,' said Selim, 'you cannot believe how quick I will be.'

'Right.' Owen put his hands on the edge of the cistern and braced himself. 'Get hold of me.'

In the background, he heard Selim say to one of the constables:

'Abdul, you stand by me with your truncheon!'

'If I strike, it will make them angry.'

'If you strike, you've got to strike them dead!'

'But, Selim,' said the worried voice, 'it is not easy to kill a snake. Not in one blow. It would be better if you just caught hold of them and threw them.'

'Thank you very much, Abdul,' said Selim.

'Selim!' said Owen sternly. 'Do it the way I told you!'

Just then a girl ducked under the legs of the cordon and came up beside Owen.

'What are you doing with our snakes?' she said fiercely.

'I'm trying to get him out . . . *Your* snakes, did you say? Who the hell are you?'

'I'm Abu's daughter.'

'He's the snake catcher,' said someone.

Light dawned.

'They're your snakes?'

'Yes.' The girl looked down over the edge. 'What's he doing down there?'

'Never mind that. Can you get him out?'

'Of course.'

She swung her leg up on the edge.

'What about the snakes?'

'I've milked the cobras.'

'Milked?'

She bent down, seized one of the snakes by the neck and held it up for Owen to see. It opened its jaws.

'See?'

The snake's mouth looked much like any other snake's mouth to Owen but he didn't feel inclined to examine it closely.

'Er . . . yes,' he said.

The cobra tried to snap at him but the girl was holding it too firmly.

'Selim,' said Abdul's worried voice, 'shall I strike?'

The girl tossed the snake back into the cistern and then dropped down after it. Owen saw her flinging the snakes aside. She put her hands under McPhee's armpits and lifted his shoulders.

'Can you take him?'

Owen grabbed hold of him. Selim, bold, reached over and caught up McPhee's legs.

They lifted him down to the ground.

Something moved under his shirt. A snake put its head out. The girl plucked it out and threw it nonchalantly into the cistern.

'It's the warmth,' she said. 'They like to go where it's warm.'

'Warm?' said Owen, and dropped on his knees.

McPhee was still alive. Alive, but very unconscious. Owen tipped his head back and looked at his eyes.

The girl knelt down beside him.

'He's overdone it, if you ask me,' she said. 'Taken a bit too much this time.'

'Someone else gave it him,' said Owen harshly.

He tore open McPhee's shirt and put an ear to his chest. A strong, snaky smell, a mixture of snake and palm oil and spices, clung to the shirt. The girl caught it, too, and looked puzzled.

The heartbeat was slow but regular. Owen looked around. The tiny yard was packed to overflowing. He was suddenly conscious of the extreme heat and lack of air.

'We must get the Bimbashi to the hospital,' he said.

There were no arabeahs in that part of the city so the constables improvised a litter out of some of the planks lying against the wall. They had just pushed their way out into the street when the owner came rushing after them.

'Hey!' he said. 'What are you doing? You can't take those!'

'Mean bastard!' said the crowd indignantly.

The owner stepped back and hurriedly changed tack.

'It's not seemly,' he said. 'He's a Bimbashi, after all!'

This was an argument which weighed with the crowd. And with the constables, who stopped uncertainly and lowered the litter to the ground.

'Come on,' said Owen, 'we've got to get a move on.'

The crowd, however, now grown to even larger proportions, would not be moved. A lively debate ensued, the outcome of which was that an *angareeb*, the universal bed, was produced and McPhee laid gently upon it. The whole crowd then accompanied them to the hospital, which Owen could have done without.

'But what was he doing there?' asked Garvin.

'I'll ask him when he wakes up,' said Owen.

McPhee, having awoken, did not respond at once. He seemed to be thinking about it.

'I don't think I can say, old man,' he said at last, rather stuffily, 'I really don't think I can say.'

2

'Can't say?' said Garvin in a fury. 'Get him here!'

McPhee insisted on standing to attention. This irked Owen because he did not know how to do it properly. He had been, such were the ways of the British Administration, a schoolmaster before being translated into a senior post in the police. Owen had been in the army in India before coming to Egypt and while this was something he now tried to forget, it still irritated him mildly to see what looked like a parody of military drill. McPhee, however, was determined to take his medicine like a man.

'I would prefer, sir, to regard the matter as closed,' he said pompously.

'Closed?' said Garvin, affecting to fall back in his chair with astonishment. 'Found drugged up to the eyeballs? Regards the matter as closed?'

'I accept that I am to blame, sir. I take full responsibility.'

'You mean you took the drug knowingly?'

McPhee was a great stickler for the truth.

'I wouldn't go so far as to say that, sir,' he said uncomfortably.

'Then what do you mean, you take responsibility?'

'I shouldn't have put myself in the position, sir,' said McPhee, hot and bothered.

'What position?'

'I – I'd rather not say, sir.'

Garvin sighed.

'McPhee,' he said, 'you are the Deputy Commandant of Police. You are found in a backyard heavily drugged.

Does it not occur to you that some might regard this as anomalous?'

'It was in off-duty hours, sir.'

'You were doing this as a recreation?'

'Yes, sir.'

'Taking the drug?'

'No, no, no, no, sir.'

'Then?'

'I don't think they meant any harm, sir.'

'Enough to knock you out for thirty-six hours? No harm?'

'I think it was just that they didn't want me to see anything.'

'McPhee,' said Garvin dangerously, 'what was it exactly that you were doing?'

McPhee was silent.

'You can tell us about it, old chap,' said Owen, trying to be helpful. 'We understand about such things.'

'What things?' said Garvin.

'Bad women,' prompted Owen gently.

'Bad women?' said Garvin incredulously.

'Bad women?' said McPhee, looking puzzled.

'Sorry!' said Owen. 'It was just that I thought –'

'Really, Owen!' said McPhee in tones of disgust.

'You're obsessed, Owen,' said Garvin. 'Keep out of it. McPhee, what were you doing there?'

'I was attending a Zzarr, sir,' said McPhee bravely.

'A Zzarr!'

'In my own time. Off duty.'

'I should bloody hope so,' said Garvin.

'What *is* a Zzarr?' asked Owen.

'A casting out of devils. From a woman.'

'They're held in secret,' said McPhee. 'You don't come across them very often.'

'Especially if you're a man,' said Garvin. 'Did you say you were *attending* one?'

'Yes, sir.'

'I thought no men were allowed?'

21

'They're not, sir. Usually.'

'Then how did you come to be there?'

'I — I invited myself, sir.'

'Using your position as Deputy Commandant?'

'Yes, sir. I'm afraid so, sir.'

'Why?'

'Just interest. Curiosity, sir. You see, sir, they happen so rarely. At least, one comes across them so rarely. Little is known about them. There's nothing about them in Lane, for instance. So —'

'You thought you would add to the world's knowledge?'

'Yes, sir. In a way.'

'Deputy Commandant!' said Garvin disgustedly. 'Casting out devils!'

'My interest was purely scientific, sir,' said McPhee stiffly.

'Oh yes. I dare say.'

McPhee's enthusiasm for traditional Egyptian ceremonies and rituals, the deeper mysteries, as he called them, was well known.

'Did it occur to you,' asked Garvin bitterly, 'that your presence there might become known? Would, in fact, certainly become known by just about everyone in Cairo? Blazoned abroad in every newspaper?'

'No, sir,' said McPhee, hanging his head.

'Listen,' said Garvin: 'how many British officers are there in the police, all told?'

'Two, sir. Not counting Owen.'

'Just you and me. Controlling a city the size of Cairo. How do we do it?'

'Well, sir,' said McPhee, slightly puzzled, 'we can call on our men. Good men, sir, fine chaps . . . the army . . .'

'Bluff!' said Garvin emphatically. 'We run the country by bluff. If somebody called our bluff we wouldn't last five minutes. We survive,' said Garvin, 'only by means of credibility. Credibility! How much bloody credibility do you think we'll have left when it gets about that we spend our time casting out devils?'

'It was off duty,' said Owen.

'Thank you, Owen. You're quite right. I have to speak precisely when there are lawyers, of the barrack-room sort, around. That we spend our *spare* time casting out devils.'

'It won't happen again,' said McPhee.

'I'm not sure I can afford the chance of it happening again.'

'No, sir,' said McPhee. 'I understand, sir.'

'I can't afford my Deputy Commandant behaving like a bloody fool,' said Garvin. 'I can't even afford him *looking* like a bloody fool.'

'No, sir.'

'I don't think you're being entirely fair,' protested Owen. 'McPhee has been the victim of an assault. It's hardly his fault.'

'Well, in a way, you know, I'm afraid it *is*,' said McPhee, honest to a fault. 'I shouldn't have been there.'

'How did you come to be drugged?'

'They gave me a drink.'

'And you drank it?'

'I thought it was hospitality,' muttered McPhee.

Garvin groaned.

'The principal reason for sacking you,' he said, 'is that you are so damned stupid.'

'I thought it was part of the ceremony,' said McPhee. 'Other people were drinking, too,' he said defiantly.

'They put something in when it got to you,' said Garvin dismissively.

'I would vouch for their honesty,' said McPhee.

'That confirms,' said Garvin, 'my view of your judgement.'

'McPhee's only just got out of sickbay,' said Owen.

McPhee was, in fact, looking distinctly wan. Garvin let Owen lead him away. He took him out to the front of the building and found an arabeah, one of the small, horse-drawn carriages that were common in Cairo. He told one of the orderlies to get in with him and see he got safely home to bed.

When he got back to his office, Nikos said: 'Garvin wants to see you.'

'He's just seen me.'

'He wants to see you again.'

'McPhee's not well,' he said to Garvin.

'It was a big dose,' said Garvin. 'It must have been, for him to be out that long.'

'It could have killed him.'

'Yes,' said Garvin, 'and that's another reason not to regard the incident as closed.'

Owen shrugged.

'Is it sensible to carry it any further? Wouldn't it be better to leave it alone and hope everyone forgets it?'

'McPhee's been the victim of an assault,' Garvin pointed out. 'You said that yourself.'

'Well . . . all right, then. Perhaps someone ought to look into it.'

'Fine!' said Garvin. 'Tell me how you get on.'

'Hey! You're not asking me to do it, are you?'

'You surely don't expect McPhee to investigate himself?'

'It's not political.'

The Mamur Zapt concerned himself only with the political. He was the equivalent of what back in England would be head of the political branch of the CID. He was, however, also much more. The Mamur Zapt had traditionally – for many centuries, indeed – been the ruler's right-hand man, the chief of his secret police, the means by which he maintained himself in power. If he was so lucky. Caliphs came, Khedives went, but the Mamur Zapt went on forever.

Even when the British had come, thirty years before, the Khedive had insisted on retaining the post. Without it, he felt nervous. The British had agreed, insisting only that they nominate the occupant of the post. That, of course, had slightly changed matters. Formally, the

Mamur Zapt, with his control of Cairo's vast network of informers, spies and underground agents, was still responsible to the Khedive. In actual fact, he was responsible to the Head of the British Administration, the British Consul-General.

If, that is, he was responsible to anybody, which Consul-General, Khedive, Khedive's Ministers, Opposition Members, Nationalists, British Government, Commander-in-Chief (British) of the army (Egyptian) and Garvin sometimes felt inclined to doubt.

All crime other than political was the responsibility not of the police, under the French-style system of law which operated in Egypt, but of the Department of Prosecutions of the Ministry of Justice, the Parquet, as it was known.

'You're not suggesting the Parquet handle this?' said Garvin, aghast. 'Investigating a British officer? A member of the Administration? Oh dear, no!' He shook his head. 'I don't think we could have that. It would set an undesirable precedent. The C-G wouldn't like it. The people at home wouldn't like it. Goodness me, no. They wouldn't like it at all.'

'We are not investigating McPhee, surely!' Owen protested.

'Well, perhaps not directly,' Garvin admitted. 'It's more the circumstances.'

'I don't call that political.'

Garvin raised his eyebrows.

'Setting up a member of the British Administration? Not political? If that's not political,' said Garvin, 'what is?'

'No, really, Owen, he's determined to get rid of me!' said McPhee heatedly. 'He's been out to get me ever since they transferred him from Alexandria. I was in charge when he arrived, just temporarily, of course, and he didn't like the way I was doing things.'

'Well –'

McPhee held up his hand.

'I know what you're going to say. Perhaps we weren't

the most efficient of outfits. But is that so bad, Owen, is it really so bad? People knew where they were. They knew what to expect. A way that is traditional, Owen, is a way that is invested with a lot of human experience. You discard it at your peril.'

'True. On the other hand –'

'I know what you are going to say. Not all tradition is good. The courbash, for instance.'

'Well, yes.'

The courbash was the traditional Egyptian whip. One of the first acts of the British Administration had been to abolish flogging.

'Well, of course, I'm not against abolishing the use of the courbash. It was a humane measure carried out for humane motives. But not all reform is like that. Sometimes it's carried out for piffling, mean little reasons. To improve efficiency, for instance. I ask you, where would we be if everything we did was subjected to that criterion?'

Not here, thought Owen. Neither you nor, probably, I.

'It's so mean-spirited. He looks around at the richness of life and then talks about efficiency!'

'He's got to run a police force, after all.'

'But why doesn't he run it in a way people want?'

'What do they want?'

'Humanity,' said McPhee, 'not efficiency.'

'I dare say. Look, I don't think he's particularly out to get you. In fact, it's the other way round. He thinks somebody is trying to set you up and he wants to stop them.'

'Who on earth would want to set me up? Garvin apart, that is.'

'You're a senior figure in the police. Lots of people. People you've arrested.'

'They don't blame me. The common criminal is a decent chap.'

Owen sighed.

'In Cairo, at any rate,' said McPhee defensively. 'Anyway, he doesn't blame me, he blames fate.'

'You don't think he might personalize fate a little?'

'No one's out to set me up,' said McPhee firmly. 'It's just another of Garvin's fantasies.'

'Some things do need explaining, though. How you finished up in the snake pit, for instance.'

'I don't think that was anything to do with the witch,' said McPhee.

'Witch?'

Oh dear, thought Owen.

'Osman told me,' said McPhee.

'That there was going to be a Zzarr?'

'Yes.'

'And he invited you to it?'

'No, no. Quite the reverse. He didn't want me to come. In fact, he was most unwilling to talk about it.'

'But he did?'

'I prised it out of him. He had come, you see, to ask me for time off. To prepare for a ceremony, he said. Well, naturally, I asked what sort of ceremony. To do with a female cousin, he said. A circumcision, I asked? At first he said yes, but then it transpired the girl was twenty so I knew he couldn't be telling the truth. In the end I got him to confess. It was a Zzarr. His sister was suffering from a mild case of possession. At least, that's what they thought. A Zzarr, I said! My goodness me!' He looked at Owen. 'They're immensely rare, you know. I've heard of them before and, indeed, once I nearly came upon one. So when I heard about this one I was tremendously excited and demanded that he tell me where it was being held.'

I'll have a word with Osman, Owen said to himself.

'It was in one of those houses on the edge of the Gama-liya, a big old house with both an outer courtyard and an inner one.'

'Could you show it me?'

'Well, I suppose I could. But I'd rather not. They placed me on my honour, you see –'

'They also drugged you.'

'Well . . . I'm not sure they did. Someone did, certainly. But not them. I was there on a basis of trust. Which was mutual.'

'You made a bargain with them?'

McPhee hesitated.

'Well, not initially.' He looked uncomfortable. 'There was, I'm afraid, an element of deception. On my part. I told them, you see, that it was a police raid. I pretended to have men with me. I demanded to see what was happening. They said it was out of the question. Very well then, I said, I will have to call my men. There was a bit of humming and ha-ing but eventually they said I could take a look through a window. I did and, my goodness me, Owen, it was fascinating! A ring of women, robes, candles, dancing –'

'And then?' Owen prompted.

'Then all the candles went out. There was a great hub-bub and lots of people came jostling me and told me I had to leave. And then the priestess came out –'

'Priestess?'

'Aalima. The witch. Well, I call her a priestess because, really, it was all most religious. It does have a religious basis, you know, Owen, there were religious sheikhs there, not in the Zzarr itself, of course, but in the courtyard outside –'

'The Aalima?' prompted Owen.

'A most striking lady, Owen, most striking. Well, at first she absolutely refused. Said it was completely out of the question. And then I said that in that case I would have to arrest them.'

'On what grounds?'

'Causing a disturbance. The sheikhs didn't like that, I can tell you.'

'The sheikhs? You threatened to arrest the sheikhs?'

Oh Christ, thought Owen.

'It was a bluff. And then I cunningly said that all I wanted to do was make sure that nothing untoward was happening, so I would be quite satisfied if they just brought me a chair and let me watch for a bit and satisfy myself on that score. In the end they agreed, provided I just listened – the music was marvellous, Owen, cymbals, you know, dubertas, timbrels. I agreed, of course, but then –'

He looked shamefaced.

'I peeped.'

'You did?'

'Yes, I'm afraid I did. And, you know, Owen, it was most interesting, for what I saw –'

'How did you come to get drugged?'

'They brought me drink. They brought everyone in the courtyard drink. It was part of it, you see –'

'Who brought you drink?'

'A most charming girl. Dressed in white virginal robes –'

'Yes, yes. Was she part of the, well, witch's entourage?'

'Yes. She came out with the bowl and took it round.'

'She gave everyone a drink?'

'Yes. Which is why, Owen,' McPhee said with emphasis, 'the drug must have been administered on a different occasion.'

'Such as?'

'Well, I can't actually think –' McPhee admitted.

'Unless, of course, she put something special in just before she got to you.'

'Oh, no, Owen. Really! A girl of integrity.'

Owen was beginning to see an argument for Gavin's position.

'And then you fell asleep?' he said.

'Yes. You know, Owen –'

'Yes?'

'I *was* very tired that night. You don't think I could have just fallen asleep in the ordinary way and that afterwards someone administered –?'

'While you were asleep? That strength? No,' said Owen.

'You see, I feel sure the lady was genuine.'

'Well,' said Owen soothingly, 'perhaps, in her way, she was.'

McPhee looked pleased.

'You think so? I must say, I've had doubts myself. Could it be a genuine survival, I've asked myself? Or –'

'I shall want to know about the people in the courtyard,' Owen said.

'Hangers on,' McPhee said, 'excluded from the real mysteries.'

'All men?'

'Yes. They're fascinated, too, of course. Can't keep away. But frightened! The Aalima is a pretty compelling figure.'

'Could you identify any of them?'

'I might be able to recognize them. They'll be local, of course.'

'If you could just give me a start . . .'

McPhee nodded.

'I'll do my best. But, Owen,' he said sternly, 'there must be no messing about with the ladies. The Zzarr is a remarkable institution. It is, I am sure, pre-Islamic. I wouldn't be surprised if it owed something to the Greek mysteries. I thought I caught some Greek words. Some Roman influence, too, perhaps. After all –'

'Yes?'

'*Bacchantium instar mulieres vidimus.*'

'Quite,' said Owen.

'I protest,' said Sheikh Musa.

'I quite agree,' said Owen heartily, 'and I join myself in your protest.'

'Wait a minute,' said the Sheikh, 'you're the man I'm protesting *to*.'

'If the subject of your protest is what I think it is,' said Owen, 'the deplorable assault on the Bimbashi a couple of nights ago, then we are on common ground.'

'It's not the assault I'm bothered about,' said the Sheikh. 'It's his presence there in the first place.

30

'At the Zzarr?'

The Sheikh winced.

'We don't like to use that word. The ceremony, you know, is not entirely regular. It's not something that's, well, officially recognized. We know it goes on, of course. There are people who, not to put too fine a point on it, are drawn to such things. I dare say you know the kind of people I mean?'

Owen, thinking of McPhee, said he did.

'I wouldn't want to encourage them by letting them think they have my approval. So I would prefer, if you don't mind, not to use the word. To do so would be to admit that I know about such things.'

'Well, yes, but . . . then why are you here?'

'I have come to lodge a formal protest at Bimbashi McPhee's presence.'

'At what?'

'An unspecified event in the Gamaliya district.'

'You can't protest at his presence if you're unable to say what he was present at!'

'From my point of view,' said the Sheikh, 'the protest is the important thing, not the event.'

'I see.'

'There's a lot of feeling in the Gamaliya about the incident.'

'I see.'

'Which might boil over.'

'What do you expect me to do about it?'

The Sheikh looked surprised.

'Nothing,' he said. 'I just wanted to lodge a protest, that was all.'

Owen understood. The Sheikh was anxious to guard his back in terms of relations with his flock.

He thought for a moment.

'I don't know that I can accept a formal protest,' he said. 'If there wasn't an event, there can't have been a presence at it.'

'Oh!'

31

'I don't think I could offer an apology. Formal, that is. However, I might be willing to issue a general statement deploring recent events – unspecified, of course, – in the Gamaliya. Would that help?'

'From my point of view, yes.'

'And from my point of view? Would that be enough to head off trouble?'

'I doubt it,' said Sheikh Musa.

Owen felt like kicking McPhee's backside.

Owen still had hopes it would all quietly fade away. The heat would surely dissuade potential troublemakers from causing a riot and by the time the hot spell was over, with luck they would have forgotten about it. As for Garvin and McPhee, Garvin would soon be departing on leave. He usually liked to return to his old haunts at Alexandria and go duck shooting. With luck, he would return in a less savage frame of mind. Perhaps McPhee, too, could be induced to take a break: go and look at some of the monasteries in Sinai, for example. In heat like this people tended to get things out of perspective.

He had better watch that this didn't happen in his own case. Perhaps he should take a holiday, too? The trouble was that Zeinab would insist on going to Paris. She regarded everywhere else as boringly provincial. The Government, on the other hand, insisted that its employees take their leave locally. Perhaps, on second thoughts, it might be best not to take a holiday. Besides, if Garvin and McPhee were away, someone had to look after the shop.

However, he must certainly guard against getting things out of perspective. He ought to take it easy for a bit. Working on this theory, he stepped out of the office mid-morning and went to his favourite café, taking the next day's newspapers or, at least, the Arabic, French and English ones with him. He could always pretend that it was work. One of the Mamur Zapt's duties was control of the press, a necessary function (in the view of the British) in a city of more than a dozen religions, a score of nationalities, a hundred different ethnic flavours and over a thousand sects, half of which at any given time were at the throats of the other half. To this end, he received advance copies of all publications.

Control, though, was another matter. Debate in the Arab world tended to be conducted at voice top anyway, and in the press the normal temperature was feverish. Cairo had taken to newspapers late but with gusto and there were hundreds of them. Each faction had at least two newspapers (two, because any group in Cairo could be guaranteed to split at least two ways) and they vied with each other in the extremity of their views and the vehemence with which they expressed them. Even the weather reports were fiercely disputed.

How to distinguish the normal incandescent from the potentially explosive? Owen usually did not try. After a year or two's experience he developed a sixth sense which alerted him to passages likely to bring rival communities to blows. The rest he left well alone, on the assumption that readers were more interested in the violence of rhetoric than in the violence of action: an approach, however, which his superiors did not always understand.

The real value of the newspapers (to Owen) was that beneath the hyperbole it was sometimes possible to detect new concerns and growth of feeling. They were sometimes, despite everything, a useful source of intelligence. Another, of course, was the gossip of Cairo's café culture. What better, then, than to combine the two? Where better for the Mamur Zapt, the Head of Political Intelligence, to sit than in a well-populated Arab café with all his intelligence material to hand? So, at least, argued Owen; and turned to the sports pages.

He became aware of someone trying covertly to attract his attention. It was a man at an adjoining table. His face seemed familiar, although it took a little while for Owen to place him. Not one of his agents but a man who sometimes gave his agents useful information. A Greek, with the dark suit and pot-like red tarboosh of the Effendi, or office worker.

'Have you heard about Philipides?' he said.

'Philipides?'

'He's coming out tomorrow.' Misunderstanding Owen's puzzlement, he said: 'It may not be in the Arab papers. It's in the Greek ones.'

'What's special about Philipides?' asked Owen.

The man smiled, obviously thinking Owen was playing with him.

'The Mamur Zapt, of all people, should know that,' he said.

He put some milliemes out for the waiter.

'Garvin ought to be interested,' he said. 'Or so they say.'

He went off through the tables. Owen sipped his coffee and searched his memory. The name meant nothing to him.

On the other side of the street he saw someone he knew and waved to him. The man waved back and came across. His name was Georgiades. Another Greek, but this time definitely not an Effendi. No tarboosh, an open-necked shirt, casual, crumpled cotton trousers held up by a belt over which his stomach bulged uncomfortably. He pointed proudly to it.

'See that?' he said. 'Another notch! Rosa's cutting down on the food. It's been a struggle for her. All Greek women are taught to fatten their husbands up but she's decided she's had enough. It's fattening the goose for killing, she says. She and her grandmother are at loggerheads again over it.'

He sat down at Owen's table and mopped his brow. There were dark patches of sweat beneath his armpits, on his chest, on his back and even on the thighs of his trousers.

'Does the name Philipides mean anything to you?' said Owen.

The Greek thought for a bit, then nodded.

'Why?'

'I don't know,' said Owen, 'but someone's just told me the Mamur Zapt, above all, ought to know. Above all. That's why I'm wondering.'

'Ah, yes,' said Georgiades, 'but which Mamur Zapt?'

'What do you mean?'

'You or your predecessor?'

'There was a gap,' said Owen. 'McPhee stood in.'

'No,' said Georgiades. 'Before.'

'There was something about corruption, wasn't there?'

'There was.'

'And Philipides was something to do with it?'

'That's right.'

'Can you give me some details?'

Georgiades considered.

'I think perhaps you ought to ask Garvin,' he said.

3

'Philipides?' said Garvin, musing. 'So he's out, is he?'

'Does it interest you?'

'Not much. They've all got to come out sometime.'

'My informant thought it should interest you.'

Garvin shrugged.

'I can't think why.'

'Is there a chance he might be looking for revenge?'

'I put him inside, certainly. But he can hardly complain about that. He was as crooked as they come.'

'Is there any reason for him to have a particular grudge against you?'

'Not really. The Parquet handled it all. I was just one of the witnesses. Mind you, I set the traps.'

'Perhaps that was it.'

'I wouldn't have thought so. There was nothing special about it.'

'It caught him,' Owen pointed out.

'I've caught lots of people,' said Garvin. 'That doesn't mean to say they all want revenge. No, if there was anyone who wanted to get his own back, it wouldn't be him.'

'Who would it be, then?'

'His boss.'

'Who was?'

Garvin grinned.

'Guess,' he suggested.

'The Mamur Zapt?'

'You've been talking to someone.'

'Georgiades. He suggested I talk to you!'

Garvin was amused.

'Prudent fellow,' he said.

'What's it all about?'

'It's straightforward, really. It was not long after I moved here from Alexandria. There was a lot to sort out. My God, you'd never believe how much there was, they were back in the last century —'

'McPhee here then?'

'No, that was later. He came *because* of this. Anyway, one day I got home and found a small parcel on the hall table. I opened it and found a pair of diamond earrings. I was a bit surprised, thought my wife had been buying things; hell, we hadn't got much money in those days, so I asked her about it when she got back. She didn't know anything about the parcel. Anyway, I asked around and found that it had been brought by one of Philipides's orderlies. So the next morning I had Philipides in and asked him about it. He said, big mistake, it was meant for someone else, the orderly had got confused. Anyway, I let him have the earrings back and thought no more about it.'

'And what was Philipides at this time?'

'He was a police inspector in the Abdin district and had the name of being the Mamur Zapt's right-hand man. I didn't put the two together though till some months later when I heard that one of my own officers had been pawning his wife's jewellery to raise money to purchase promotion. Well, as you can imagine, I had him in. It took a bit of time but eventually I got from him that Philipides was demanding the money as the price of the Mamur Zapt's recommendation.'

Garvin looked at Owen.

'It was significant in those days. The Commandant then was Wainwright and he didn't have a clue. The Mamur Zapt just twisted him round his finger. What the Mamur Zapt said, went. Well, I was pretty shocked, I can tell you. I hadn't realized things were as bad as that. I made some discreet inquiries and found that it was quite an accepted practice. But what the hell was I to do?'

'If the officer had confessed –'

Garvin gestured impatiently.

'Yes, but, you see, I couldn't go to Wainwright. I was just a new boy in those days and Deputy Commandant carried no clout. Wainwright took the Mamur Zapt's word on everything.'

'Yes, but if you had the evidence –'

'It wasn't enough. If it came to it, the Mamur Zapt could disown Philipides. Say it was nothing to do with him. I had to show there was a connection between the two.'

'So how did you do it?'

'Set a trap. I told the original officer to let Philipides know that he had confessed to me and then I tapped the telephone lines between Philipides and the Mamur Zapt.'

'Telephone?' The telephone system in Cairo was still in its infancy and largely consigned to Government offices; at the time Garvin was referring to, it would have been younger still.

'Yes,' Garvin replied, 'The Mamur Zapt had one of the earliest ones.'

'Did it work?'

'Up to a point, yes. Philipides rang him that afternoon and said enough to incriminate the pair of them. I took it all down and showed it to Wainwright the next morning.'

He walked over to the window and poured himself some water from the earthenware pitcher which stood next to the shutters of all Cairo offices where it would cool.

'Even then it wasn't simple,' he said. 'Wainwright just wouldn't believe me. I had to go to the Consul-General. Over his head. That made me popular, I can tell you! In the end, I got the C-G to agree but it took three weeks to persuade Wainwright to suspend the two.'

'By which time –'

'No, they couldn't very well destroy the evidence. They tried intimidation first, put a lot of pressure on the officer.

I had to give him an armed guard. I was terrified he would give way. They tried it on me, too.'

Owen smiled.

'Yes, well, that didn't get them very far,' said Garvin. 'But it was pretty unpleasant. I carried a gun with me all the time. Then they tried to discredit me. They dredged up the earrings. Said that I was in the habit of accepting presents and only made a fuss this time because I wanted more. Fortunately, I'd told Judge Willis all about it the day it happened. It just shows you can't be too careful.'

He pushed the shutters slightly apart to encourage a breeze. Normally they kept the offices dark and cool but the prolonged hot spell had made them like ovens.

'Next, they said it was political.'

'Political!'

'Yes. They said it was all a trick to get Egyptians out and British in. They made great play of that when it came to the trial, and the Parquet was content to let it run because they wanted to make their own political point. They gave me a real grilling. Went on for days. Apart from the officer, and he was my subordinate, I was the chief witness, you see. To the telephone conversation, anyway, and that was crucial, because it was only that, really, that tied the Mamur Zapt in. In the end, though, it suited them to go for a conviction.'

'Which they got.'

'Yes. Well, I say "got". Both were found guilty and sent to jail but the Mamur Zapt was released almost at once on compassionate grounds. He knew too much about all the people involved. The politicians were dead scared that if they didn't look after him, he would spill all the beans.'

'Where is he now?'

'Enjoying a fat pension in Damascus.'

'It sounds as if he's got it all worked out,' said Owen. 'I'll bear his example in mind.'

'There are other examples, too, you might bear in mind,' said Garvin. 'Wainwright got the push shortly after. I got promotion.'

'Thank you. What about McPhee?'

'That bum!'

'How does he come into it?'

'Well, they needed a replacement as Mamur Zapt. The one thing he had to be, in the circumstances, was honest.'

'Well, he is that,' said Owen.

'I managed to get it made temporary. The price was that when they filled the post he got moved sideways to Deputy Commandant. I'm trying to make that,' said Garvin, 'temporary, too.'

In this hot weather, Owen liked to sleep outside. He had a small garden, which the house's previous occupant, a Greek, had developed in the Mediterranean style rather than the English, more for shade than colour. It was thick with shrubs but there was a little open space beneath a large orange tree and it was here that Owen disposed his bed, not too far in under the branches in case creepy-crawlies dropped on him during the night, but not too far out, either, where the moonlight might prevent him from sleeping.

This morning he awoke with the sun, as he always did, and at once reached his hand down for his slippers, tapping them automatically on the ground to dislodge any scorpion that might have crept in. Then he slipped them on and made for the shower. The water came from a tank in the roof and was still warm from the previous day's sun. He was just reaching out happily for the soap when he heard the slither behind him and froze. Out of the corner of his eye he saw the tail disappearing into the wall.

'Jesus!' he said, and dispensed with the shower for that morning.

The snake catcher came that afternoon. He was a gnarled, weather-beaten little man with snake bites all over his hands and carrying a leather bag and a cane.

'Another one?' he said. 'It's the hot weather that's bringing them out.'

'I didn't see what sort it was,' said Owen, 'I just caught a glimpse of the tail.'

He took the snake catcher to the showerhouse and pointed out the hole. The snake catcher sniffed at it and said: 'Yes, that's the way he came, but he doesn't live there.'

He went round to the back of the showerhouse and showed Owen the hole where the snake had got out. A slight, almost imperceptible track led into the undergrowth.

'Not been doing much gardening, have you?' said the snake catcher. 'He's all right in there.'

He followed the trail in carefully.

'There he is!' he said suddenly. 'See him? Down by that root.'

It would be just the head and eyes that were visible. Owen couldn't see anything.

The snake catcher stood and thought a bit. He was working out where the tail was.

After a while he put down the leather bag beside Owen and circled round behind the snake. This was the tricky part, he had told Owen on a previous occasion. The next bit was more obviously dramatic but this bit was tricky because the tail would often be coiled around roots or undergrowth and it was not always easy to tear it loose.

Owen liked to watch a craftsman at work. He took up a position where he could see.

The snake catcher began to move cautiously into the undergrowth, peering intently before him. He came to a stop and just stood there for a while, looking.

Suddenly, he pounced. The snake came up with his hand, wriggling and twisting. He threw it out into the open. It tried at once to squirm away but he cut off its escape by beating with his cane. The snake came to ground in the middle of the clearing.

The snake catcher crept forward and then suddenly brought the cane down hard on the snake's neck, pressing it in to the ground. Then, holding the cane down with his left hand, he reached out with his right hand and seized the snake with thumb and forefinger, forcing the jaws open. He dropped the cane and held out the skirts of his galabeah so that the snake could strike at them. He let it strike several times. Yellow beads of venom appeared on the cloth. When he was satisfied that all the poison had been drawn, he opened his bag and dropped the cobra inside. Snake catchers hardly ever killed their snakes.

'What will you do with it?'

'Dispose of it through the trade. Some shops want them. Charmers. Some people buy them for pets.'

'You'd need to know what you're doing.'

'Most people don't,' he said. 'That's why there's always a demand for new ones. They die easy.'

'It's not the other way round? The owners that die?'

'We take the fangs out first. That makes them safe. The poison flows along the fang, you see. The trouble is, they use the teeth for killing their food. Once they're gone, they don't last very long.'

'What about milking?' asked Owen, displaying his new-found knowledge.

'It's all right if you know what you're doing. There is a sac behind the fangs where the poison is. You let it strike – that's what I was doing – until the sac is drained dry. Then you're all right for about a fortnight.'

'If you had a lot of snakes,' said Owen, thinking about the cistern where they had found McPhee, 'you'd have to know each one.'

'Well, you would know each one, wouldn't you, if it was your job.'

They walked back to the house.

'Do you know a snake catcher over in Gamaliya?'

'There are several. Which one?'

'He's on the Place of Tombs side.'

'Abu?'

'That's the one. He's got a daughter.'

The snake catcher smiled.

'He's got a right one there!' he said.

'She seems to know a lot about it.'

'Oh, she knows a lot about it, all right. She wants to be one of us. Take on from him after he's gone, like. But it won't do. She's a girl, isn't she? We're a special sect, you know. The Rifa'i. You've got to be one of us before you're allowed to do it. It's very strict. Got to be, hasn't it? And we don't have women. It would confuse the snakes. Anyway, it's not a woman's job.'

'How come she knows so much about it?'

'Watched her dad. He let her see too much, in my opinion. He wanted a boy, you see, and then when one didn't come he got in the habit of treating her as one.'

'Well, she seems a lively girl.'

'Yes, but who'd want a daughter like that? What a business when it came to marrying her off! You might have to pay her husband extra.'

When Owen arrived at her *appartement*, Zeinab wasn't there. She arrived half an hour later.

'Well, what do you expect?' she said. 'If you think I'm going to be waiting for you half naked in bed every time you drop in, you'd better think again.'

Zeinab had, unfortunately, not forgotten the business about the girl. It had been a mistake telling her. For some obscure reason she blamed him.

'And, incidentally, what happened to that diamond?'

Owen fished in his pocket and took it out. Zeinab inspected it critically.

'Cheap!' she pronounced. 'They've certainly got you worked out, haven't they?'

Owen put the stone back in his pocket.

'Is that a good idea?' asked Zeinab. 'Going around with it in your pocket?'

'It's all right,' Owen assured her. 'It's safer there than in the Bab-el-Khalk.'

Zeinab began to feel motherly feelings.

'Yes, I'm sure, darling. But is it a good idea all the same? Oughtn't you to give it to someone? If you keep it, you see,' she said, pronouncing the words very slowly, as to an idiot, 'they may say you've deliberately kept it.'

'I'm keeping it as evidence.'

'Yes, but –' said Zeinab, motherliness struggling against exasperation.

'I've booked it in,' Owen assured her.

'Did you book the girl in, too, while you were at it?' asked Zeinab tartly.

Owen overtook McPhee just as he was going up the first steps of the Bab-el-Khalk. He put an arm round him solicitously.

'How are you feeling, old chap?'

'Better now, thanks.'

'You still look a bit groggy.'

'I'm shaking it off. It *was* a big dose, I suppose,' McPhee admitted.

'Yes . . . and in this heat . . . Look, old chap, why don't you take a few days off? Go and look at some monasteries somewhere . . . Sinai . . .'

'I don't like –'

'I can look after it all for a few days. It would do you good. Better to shake it off completely, you know, not go on struggling against it . . . This heat.'

'Well thank you, Gareth. I'll think about it. Yes, I'll think about it.'

'It goes on, doesn't it,' he said to Garvin as they passed in the corridor, 'this heat? Could do with a bit of fresh air. Wish I was at the coast . . .'

'The coast . . .' murmured Garvin reflectively.

Getting rid of those two would get rid of half the difficulty, he told himself. By the time they came back they would have forgotten all about it. He had no intention whatsoever of trying to find out what had happened to McPhee at the Zzarr. As far as he could see, all that had happened was that they'd slipped him something to make sure he

44

didn't see what he wasn't supposed to see. It had been a bit nasty putting him in the cistern with all those snakes, though. Still, you could look at it another way, if the girl was going there regularly to milk them, she'd be bound to find him. And then, he'd have woken up anyway once the drug had worn off. Christ, what an awakening! No, the whole thing was best left alone. If, of course, it could be left alone . . .

The first indication that it couldn't came not, as he had half-expected, from rumblings in the Gamaliya but from the press. There was a paragraph in one of the fundamentalist weeklies about Christian interference in local religious rites. No details were given but the McPhee incident was obviously being referred to.

Owen was a little surprised. He had expected, following the visit from Sheikh Musa, grumblings at the local level but, given the secrecy of the event and the unwillingness of Sheikh Musa to give it publicity, he had not expected it to reach the press. A couple of days later there was another reference to it, in the Nationalist press this time and with more detail. And then a day or so after, it was picked up yet again, more fiercely, in a sectarian paper which was critical of both the offender – now named unequivocally as an Englishman – and of the local religious authorities.

It was clear that the tip-off had not come from Sheikh Musa. Who had it come from, then? Owen sat back and thought. Was there something after all in Garvin's supposition that someone was trying to set up McPhee?

This looked very like an orchestrated campaign. He thought about it a little more and then decided to test if it was by inserting a mild spoke in their wheel. He would excise all press reference to the incident for a week or two. It wouldn't stop publication entirely since there was a large and thriving underground press in Cairo, but it would force someone's hand if they were trying to mount a campaign. They would have to take the greater risk of illicit publication, and he could have the printers watched in the hope of picking up anyone new who came into the market.

It seemed to work, for after about a week the references in the press died down. He waited for the approaches to the underground printers. Then one morning he came in to the Bab-el-Khalk to find Nikos waiting for him.

'There's been an attack on a Coptic shop in the Gamaliya,' he said.

Owen hardly needed to ask where it was.

'Near the Place of Tombs? Right, I'll go there.'

The Copts, the original inhabitants of the city – they had been there long before the Muslims arrived – were Christians, and were usually the first targets of any religious unrest.

He found the shop easily enough. There was a little knot of people standing in front of it. There was no broken glass. Shops in the traditional quarters, like the houses, did not have glass windows. They were open to the street. Instead, though, there were bits of wood lying everywhere. At night, the shopkeepers drew wooden shutters across their shops and these had obviously been broken open.

He couldn't at first make out what kind of shop it was. All he could see, scattered about on the ground, were little gilt cylinders. Puzzled, he picked one up. It had three thin metal rings attached to it.

'It's for women to put on,' said the shopkeeper. 'It keeps the veil off the face.'

Seeing that Owen still did not understand – he knew little about technology and even less about female technology – he demonstrated by fitting it on himself. The cylinder went across the nose and the face veil was suspended from it. The rings held the cloth away from the nostrils and the mouth to allow passage of air.

Owen shrugged.

'At least with this sort of stuff you don't get much broken,' he said.

'It's not the damage,' said the shopkeeper. 'It's the – I'll

46

never feel the same again. We've lived here for twenty years. We thought we were liked by our neighbours. We thought we liked them. Now something like this happens!'

'It's not the neighbours, Guptos,' said one of the bystanders quietly.

'It's someone in the Gamaliya,' said the Copt bitterly. 'Don't tell me they came right across the city just to break up my shop!'

Owen went inside with him. At the back of the shop were some stairs which led to an upper storey. Some children, huddled on the stairs, peeped down at him.

'It's the effect on the kids,' said the shopkeeper. 'We've always let them run around, play with who they like. They've got friends . . . Now my wife is afraid to let them out of her sight.'

He bent down and began to pick up cylinders from the floor.

'It's not the shop I mind about,' he said. 'We can always start again. It's the kids, my wife. How can she go to the *suk* and look them in the face, knowing what they've done? What they could do again? We'll have to move.'

Owen looked around. The fittings of the shop were very simple. The walls were lined with shelves, as in a cupboard, on which the goods were stored. There was a low counter at the front on which, when a potential customer inquired, particular items could be displayed; or on which, typically, the shopkeeper would sit when he was not working. He worked on the ground behind the counter. Owen could see some tools scattered among the debris.

There was not, in fact, a lot of debris. This was not the moment to tell the man he was lucky; but he was. Owen had often seen worse. This did not look like the random, total violence that usually resulted when a mob ran amok. It was something measured, selected, perhaps, to send a message.

'Why was it you?' he asked.

'Why is it ever us?' said the shopkeeper bitterly.

'Are there other Copts in this part of the Gamaliya?'

'A few. It'll be their turn next.'

'There will be men here tonight,' said Owen. 'It won't happen again.'

'They'll be here tonight,' said the shopkeeper, 'but they won't be here every night. And it will happen again.'

He went out of his shop and began to pick up cylinders left lying in the street. The onlookers began to help him. A woman, dark-gowned, black-veiled, came up and unobtrusively placed a bowl of beans on the ground in front of the shop and then went away again.

Owen crossed to the other side of the street to look over at the shop. His foot caught something in the gutter. It was a cylinder that had rolled across. He bent down and picked it up.

One or two of the cylinders had rolled their way to this side of the street and a man came across picking them up. He took Owen's from him.

'Women's wares,' he said, turning it over in his hand dismissively.

An old man, white-galabeahed, white-turbaned and white-bearded, came stumping along the street, supporting himself with a stick. He came to a stop beside Owen.

'A bad business,' he said, gesturing across the road with his stick.

'It's always a bad business,' said Owen, 'when neighbours fall out.'

'Neighbours?' said the old man sharply. 'It wasn't neighbours who did this. Hello, Guptos!' he called across to the shopkeeper. 'A bad business, this!'

'Hello, Mohammed!' he said. 'A bad business, indeed!'

The old man limped across and embraced him.

'There you are!' he said. 'A Muslim embraces a Copt! I don't care who sees me.'

One or two of the spectators looked uneasy.

'Not too much of that, old man,' someone muttered.

The old man whirled on them.

'What's wrong with it, hey? He's one of us, isn't he?

48

Been in the Gamaliya twenty years! That's good enough, isn't it?'

'Yes, yes. Just don't overdo it, that's all.'

'You watch out, Mohammed!' someone called out. 'It'll be your shop next time!'

'Just let them try it!' shouted the old man, waving his stick. 'Just let them try it! I'll soon show them what's what!'

'It would be at night, you old fool,' said someone. 'You'd be too busy showing Leila what's what!'

There was a general laugh, in which the old man joined, and then, still excited, he was gently persuaded on his way.

'He's right, though,' someone said. 'It ought to count if you've lived here twenty years.'

'Yes,' said someone else, 'they ought to have picked one of the other Copts.'

4

'Hello, Osman,' said Owen. 'How is your sister?'

'Sister?' said the orderly. 'I haven't got a sister.'

'That's funny,' said Owen. 'You had one last week.'

Osman shook his head.

'Not me,' he said. 'You're thinking of someone else, effendi.'

'I don't think so. Didn't you tell Bimbashi McPhee that you had a sister?'

'No, effendi. It was someone else. I've never had a sister.'

'The one who was possessed by evil spirits? Who was at the Zzarr?'

Osman swallowed.

'That wasn't my sister, effendi. That was . . . my cousin. Yes, my cousin.'

'And was she cured?'

'Oh, yes, effendi, thank you very much. She's quite better now.'

'Oh good. All the same, these things recur, you know. We'd better take her along to the hospital and get the hakim there to have a look at her.'

'I don't think that will be necessary, effendi,' said Osman faintly. 'It's – it's not worth troubling the mighty hakim.'

'No trouble at all,' said Owen briskly. 'I'll arrange an appointment for her tomorrow. Now, what was her name?'

'Amina,' said the orderly in a whisper. 'Yes, Amina. I think.'

'Right. Well, I'll arrange that and let you know the time.'

'Yes, effendi,' said the orderly, worried.

Owen waited.

'Or perhaps,' he suggested, 'you haven't got a cousin either?'

'Oh, no, effendi,' said Osman hurriedly. 'I have a cousin. In fact, several.'

'Make sure,' said Owen, 'that it's the right one who turns up.'

He turned up at the hospital himself to make sure. Osman looked even more worried; indeed, aghast.

He had, however, brought a woman with him, heavily muffled in head veil and face veil and dressed in the usual shapeless black of the poor women of Cairo.

'Greetings, madam,' said Owen cheerfully. 'I am sorry to hear about your affliction. But do not worry. The hakim will soon cure you. The treatment may be a bit painful –'

The woman gave a twitch.

'– but it won't last more than a few weeks.'

The hooded figure gave Osman a look.

'Now, I just want to put a few questions to you before you go in to the hakim.'

They would have to be put through Osman, her nearest male relative, but Owen had never yet met an Egyptian woman prepared to stay silent and let the male answer on her behalf.

'First, how long have you suffered from this affliction?'

'Six years,' said Osman at random.

'Six years? Are you sure it isn't five years?'

'Six,' said Osman.

'But you haven't asked her yet.'

Osman did so now. The woman muttered something back which sounded suspiciously like 'How do I know?'

'Perhaps it was five,' said Osman.

'Quite a long time, anyway. So that all the world will

know of your affliction. There will be no doubt, then, when I ask people –'

'Ask people?' said Osman.

'Your family –'

Osman nodded but looked grim.

'The local hakim –'

Osman winced. This was going to cost him.

'The neighbours –'

Osman drew a deep breath. Things were getting out of hand.

'How sad that you should be so afflicted!' said Owen sympathetically. 'And that all the world should know! And what a price you'll have to pay,' he said to Osman, 'to get any man to take her! I'd be surprised if you could get anyone to marry her at all.' There were signs of stirring beneath the shapeless black. 'Never mind,' he said encouragingly, 'when everyone knows you've been to the English hakim to be cured of not being quite right in the head –'

'Not quite right in the head?' said the woman.

'Permanently afflicted –'

'There's nothing wrong with my head,' declared the woman firmly.

'Hush, woman!' said Osman unhappily.

'There may be with yours!'

'Don't let it worry you, Amina,' said Owen.

'Amina?' said the woman.

Back at the Bab-el-Khalk, severely cast down, Osman was ready to confess. None of his female relatives, the mock-Amina – for whom, win or lose, he had committed himself to buying a necklace – least of all, unfortunately, was possessed or weak in the head. There never had been anyone possessed. It was just a story he had made up knowing the Bimbashi's interest in such things as Zzarrs.

Even that, Owen pointed out, was untrue. He had not made the story up. Someone else had; and given it to him to use to entrap the Bimbashi.

Osman was silent. The worried lines on his forehead, however, indicated that he could see big trouble ahead.

'So who was it who spoke to you, Osman?' asked Owen pleasantly.

Osman took a deep breath.

'Effendi, I do not know.'

'What a pity you do not know!' said Owen. 'It could have saved you a lot of distress.'

'A man spoke to me in the *suk*,' tried Osman bravely.

'Whom you did not know and whom you could not recognize if you saw him again.'

'That's right, effendi,' said Osman thankfully.

'And out of the goodness of your heart you decided to entrap the Bimbashi?'

'Well, it wasn't just out of the goodness –' admitted Osman.

'How much did they pay you?'

'One hundred piastres.'

Owen looked at him severely.

'I will give it back, effendi,' said Osman despondently.

'But how will you give it back, Osman, if you don't know the man and would not recognize him if you saw him?'

'Perhaps I would recognize him,' said Osman, 'and I might see him in the *suk*.'

'Well, I'll tell you what I will do, Osman. You have raised your hand against the Bimbashi and that is a serious offence, for which I am going to send you to work in the gangs mending the levées along the river. However, I shall postpone your departure for a week or two and if meanwhile you should happen to see the man who spoke to you and are able to point him out to me I might be prepared to take things no further. Oh, and, Osman, no one need know that you had pointed him out to me.'

Osman looked at him thoughtfully.

Where, Owen asked himself, could he find out if another Zzarr was being held in the immediate future? It was not something he could discover through his usual intelligence sources. Why was that, he wondered? He suddenly realized that all his sources were to do with men. The Islamic world was severely bifurcated between a public world and a private world. The public world was occupied only by men. This was the world he knew and his agents were concerned with. It was a world rather like that of the army, in which all the players were men and all the initiatives were masculine.

Women belonged to the other world, the private world. They existed behind walls, behind closed doors. When they emerged into the public world, they carried the walls with them in the form of their black, shapeless garments and heavy veils. The Zzarr was part of that private world. Worse – from his point of view – it was part of a sub-division of that world, a sub-division from which men were excluded. There was another world within the private world which belonged to women only.

It would be no good asking his agents. They were all men. Nor could he ask the orderlies. The Zzarr was something women kept from their husbands. They might have a vague idea, but it would be at the level of rumour and gossip. He could not even go to Sheikh Musa. The religious authorities took care to keep their distance from such things. They were obliged to tolerate but could not recognize.

He remembered, a few months before, witnessing one such women's ceremony. It had taken place in a mosque, now abandoned but to which women still came for their own special purposes. The purpose of this particular ceremony had been to establish whether a child would grow up dumb. Mothers came and held their babies to a special part of the wall. If they cried – and they usually did, their mothers made damned sure of that – prospects were favourable.

The religious authorities knew very well that such practices went on. They did not condone them but knew they

54

could not stamp them out. They were part of an incredibly resilient female underworld.

About which Owen knew virtually nothing. That was all right, people were entitled to their secrets and he wasn't one to go prying into them like McPhee. Mamur Zapt he might be, but he had a decent British sense of reticence.

On the other hand, he wanted to get in touch with the person who ran the Zzarr; the witch, or whatever she was. Witch! Owen winced. That would look good in the newspapers: Mamur Zapt out hunting for witches! He could write the editorials himself.

Yes, the fact was, he had a gap in the information system. His informants were all men. He needed to have some women.

But how could he find them? Women were kept well away from him, why, he could not think, and the only one he knew at all well was Zeinab. He could ask her, but she was not exactly a person he could employ as an agent. It wasn't just that she would be certain to take a line of her own, never mind what the instructions were. The problem was that she was a member of Cairo's social elite and had far more in common with sophisticated Parisiennes than with her sisters in the *suk*.

He could ask Georgiades's Rosa, even though she was still only about fifteen. She was as sharp as a knife, an implement which she had made clear she was ready to use should her husband step out of line. Georgiades had been a changed man since his marriage. The trouble with Rosa, though, was that she was Greek. There was certainly a very strong Greek female culture. Unfortunately, it was not the same as the traditional one of the *suks*.

There was a nice girl he had recently met. In fact, she was the one he'd gone to the abandoned mosque to meet. The problem was that she was too nice. She was much too kind and gentle.

That could not be said of another of Owen's acquaintances. That gipsy girl was just the sort of person he needed.

Unfortunately, she had left town in a hurry a few weeks before, just ahead of the police.

No, it wouldn't do. He would have to recruit women by the ordinary means. Nikos handled all that side. Nikos? Women? That wasn't going to work. He would have to put aside the issue of recruiting women for the moment.

But what about the Zzarr? He mentioned it tentatively to Zeinab.

'I've no time for that superstitious stuff,' she said dismissively. 'Women are never going to get anywhere while they go on believing that sort of rubbish.'

'Gareth,' said his friend, Paul, the ADC, 'does the name Philipides mean anything to you?'

They were at a reception at the Abdin Palace. Owen, splendidly uniformed, had just mounted the grand staircase lined by the Khedival royal guard, even more splendidly uniformed and carrying lances. Owen did not greatly care for such occasions – for one thing, they served only soft drinks – but he was here at the express invitation of His Royal Highness the Khedive and one did not disregard such invitations. The British were punctilious in observing the forms of Khedival rule. Substance was another matter.

The Khedive, too, was punctilious over observance of the forms. They were all he had left.

'I think he does it just to provoke,' said Paul. 'This evening, for instance: why so splendid an occasion just to mark the arrival of the Turkish ambassador?'

'Past relationships, I suppose,' said Owen. The Khedive had once been a vassal of the Sublime Porte and Egypt was still, in the view of Constantinople, part of the Ottoman Empire.

'Past,' asked Paul, 'or future?'

'No chance,' said Owen. 'We wouldn't let him.'

'Quite so,' said Paul. 'But he *does* love to raise the spectre.'

He had taken Owen by the arm and led him behind some potted palm trees; and it was then that he asked about Philipides, and whether any of it made sense.

Owen nodded.

'Good. Because it didn't to me.'

'And now it does?'

'I have been brushing up on past history. At the C-G's request,' Paul said with emphasis.

'Why is that?'

'He thinks it's going to come up again.'

'The corruption business?'

'The Garvin business.'

'On what grounds?'

'Miscarriage of justice. They were convicted only on Garvin's word.'

'There was a police officer –'

'One of Garvin's subordinates. Coerced, so they claim.'

'Who are "they"?'

'We don't know. All we know is that the Parquet wants formally to reopen the whole affair.'

'Philipides is out,' said Owen.

'Yes. Early. I don't know if that's cause or result. Possibly it's just the pretext. Anyway, someone's using it to have a go at Garvin. And what we are beginning to think is that it's not so much Garvin they want to have a go at, it's us.'

'Garvin just a pretext, too.'

'Exactly. So, old chap, the Consul-General would like you to take a look.'

'Have you tipped off Garvin?'

'He'll soon find out. But we can't ask him to handle this. He's a material witness. Besides –'

'Yes?'

'This really is political. It really is.'

Paul caught someone's eye and went across to shake hands. *'Cher ministre,'* Owen heard him begin. Then he, too, began to do his duty, circulating less among politicians and diplomats – that was Paul's patch – than among senior civil servants and Pashas. They were all, of course, Egyptian, but the language spoken was not Egyptian Arabic.

Nor, significantly, was it English. It was French. The Egyptian elite's cultural allegiance was to France. It went to France for its education, its reading, its clothes and its vacations. It spoke French more naturally than it spoke Arabic.

When he was with Zeinab they habitually spoke French. Zeinab's father was here now on the other side of the room with a circle of his cronies. He extended a hand to greet Owen as he arrived.

'My dear boy,' he said. 'So nice to see you! You know everyone, don't you?'

They were all Pashas; like him, hereditary rulers of vast estates. Nowadays they were deeply into cotton and international finance (borrowing, mostly). They looked outward to Europe, where they spent most of their time, adjusting to the loss of power which had come with British rule. They supplied most of the Khedive's cabinet but their capacity for action, or, indeed, inaction, was severely constrained now by the presence of British Advisers at the top of each Ministry. Nevertheless, Governmental posts were much sought after, not least by Nuri, Zeinab's father, and his cronies. They belonged, however, to a previous generation; a fact to which they were by no means reconciled.

They were all known to Owen, except one.

'Demerdash Pasha,' introduced Nuri, with a wave of his band.

The Pasha bowed distantly.

'Captain Owen. The dear boy has a *tendresse* for Zeinab,' he explained.

'How is Zeinab these days?' asked one of the other Pashas.

'The Mamur Zapt,' he heard another one amplifying for the benefit of the newcomer.

Owen saw the impact.

'Mamur Zapt?'

A little later he found an opportunity to speak to Owen.

'I knew your predecessor,' he said.

'A friend?'

'We worked together. A true servant of the Khedive.'

'As I aspire to be,' said Owen.

The Pasha looked puzzled.

'How can that be?' he said.

One of the other Pashas linked arms with him affectionately.

'Demerdash Pasha has been away for a long time,' he said with a smile.

'And where have you been spending your time, Pasha?' asked Owen.

'Constantinople,' the man said shortly.

'Demerdash Pasha is a great friend of the Turks,' said one of the other Pashas.

Demerdash turned on him.

'I am not a great friend of the Turks,' he said sharply. 'I was there because the Khedive asked me to be there.'

'You are a friend of Egypt, *mon cher*,' said Nuri.

'Yes,' said Demerdash, 'a friend of Egypt. But of Egypt as she was and not as she is.'

'Oh la la,' said Nuri, and led him away.

'Just the same as he used to be,' said one of the other Pashas, watching them go. 'He doesn't give an inch.'

'Well, that's good, isn't it?' said another Pasha.

'That remains to be seen,' said the first Pasha.

The group broke up with Nuri's departure and Owen continued his circulation. Some time later, however, he found himself standing next to Nuri and Demerdash at the buffet table. They were talking to someone who had, apparently, just returned from the Sudan.

'And how were things down in the Bahr-el-Ghazal?' asked Demerdash.

The other man shrugged. 'Hot,' he said.

'What about women?'

'All right.'

'That was where the best slaves came from,' said Demerdash. 'Beautiful black ones.'

'None of that these days. They've got rid of slaves.'

Demerdash made a gesture of dismissal.

'Does it make any difference?'

'You've got to be careful.'

'The British!' said Demerdash scornfully.

'All the same –'

'Don't tell me you spent that time there without sampling at least a few little *négresses*.'

'What's that?' said Nuri.

Demerdash turned to him.

'*Il me dit qu'il a passé six ans au Sudan sans une seule petite négresse!*'

'Impossible!' said Nuri.

The table bowed under the weight of food. There were gigantic Nile perch with lemons stuffed in their jaws, pheasants cooked but then with their feathers replaced so that they looked as if they had just wandered off an autumnal English field, ducklings shaped out of foie gras, huge ox heads from which the tongues, cooked, lolled imbecilely.

Paul regarded these latter with disfavour.

'Exactly like a Parliamentary delegation,' he said sourly.

The reception finished about eleven. The night was still young by Cairo standards and many of the guests went off to revel less stiffly in more congenial places. Owen decided to walk home. The other side of rising with the light was that he declined with the light, and midnight always found him totally stupid.

Besides, the night was the best time for walking in Cairo. The city was at its coolest then. Shadow veiled the strident and the angular and cooperated with the moon to emphasize the soft shapes and arches. The lower level of the city disappeared and you suddenly became aware of the magical beauty of the upper parts of the houses, with their balconies and minarets, the fantastic woodwork of the overhanging, box-like meshrebiya windows, and the grotesque corbels which carried the first floor out over the street. Higher still and the moon revealed more clearly than in the day the delicacy of the domes and minarets of the mosques and the slender towers of the fountain houses. Everything was silvery. The moon seemed even to strike silver out of the fine, tight-packed grains of sand of the streets.

As Owen set out, an arabeah drew up alongside him. He waved it away but it stopped just in front of him determinedly.

'Hello!' said a soft female voice, which somehow seemed familiar. Suddenly he remembered.

'You again!' It was the girl he had found in his bed. 'What do you want?'

'I want you to be nice to me. And I want to be nice to you.'

'Sorry,' said Owen. 'I'm well supplied, thanks.'

'It's not like that,' she said.

'What is it like?'

'Why don't you come home with me and find out?'

'Sorry.' He shook his head. 'Someone is expecting me.'

'Zeinab's not the only girl in the world. And, anyway, she's not expecting you. She's at Samira's.'

Owen stopped, astonished. How did a girl like this know about Samira, the Princess Samira? And how did she know about Zeinab, for that matter?

'You know Samira?'

'As well as I know you. Surprisingly well.'

Owen considered the matter. He was intrigued.

But then, he was intended to be intrigued.

'No, thank you,' he said, and walked on.

Later, he was sorry. Plums, after all, do not grow on every tree.

Owen went down to the Gamaliya next day to see that things were all right. He found the shop open and the Copt busy behind the counter. The shelves, though, were half empty.

'A lot missing?' asked Owen, indicating the shelves with his hand.

'No, no. I've just not put them up. I have to take them

down at night, you see, now that the shutters have been broken. It's not worth it. The women know what they want and can always ask for it. I keep the stuff inside now.'

An idea came to Owen.

'Do you talk to the women?'

'Of course.'

'And sometimes, perhaps, you overhear things?'

'Perhaps,' said the Copt, slightly bewildered.

'Did you know about the Zzarr?'

He caught the look before the Copt's face became studiously blank.

'Zzarr? I don't think so.'

Owen smiled.

'*I* think so,' he said.

The Copt shook his head.

'The reason I am asking,' said Owen, 'is that I think the Zzarr could have something to do with the attack on your shop.'

The shopkeeper looked surprised.

'How could it?'

'Just believe me, that I think it could. Now, what I'm trying to do is stop it happening again. So I need to know.'

'I know there was a Zzarr,' said the shopkeeper. 'That's about all I know. Honestly!'

'Where was it?'

'It was in the house over there.'

'Show me.'

The Copt called into the house and a woman appeared. She was dressed in black like the other women in the street and veiled like them. The Copt told her to look after things while he was gone. He said he wouldn't be long.

'Normally she doesn't mind,' he said to Owen. 'It's just that now –'

The house was only about a couple of hundred yards away. Owen knocked on the door. No one responded.

'I think it's empty,' said the Copt.

'Who does it belong to?'

'A Mr Abbas, I think. He lives in the Gamaliya somewhere.'

There were still some policemen about. Owen set them to work finding out where Mr Abbas lived – it was simply a question of knocking on people's doors and asking, someone was bound to know. He himself went to a café to wait. The Copt, he sent back to his shop.

Eventually, one of the constables returned. Or rather, two of them returned. One was the man who found out; the other was Selim, who had now, on the strength of past glory, appointed himself Acting Sergeant, still, unfortunately, unpaid.

Mr Abbas owned a large store off one of the *suks*. He came out to meet Owen and then invited him into his office to take tea. They sat on a low leather divan and the tea was served on an equally low table, about six inches high. Courtesy demanded that it was some time before they got down to business, but eventually they did.

'My house, indeed,' said Mr Abbas blandly, 'and sometimes I let it. But a Zzarr! Oh dear, I had no idea.'

'They gave no indication of their purpose?'

'Well, of course, I don't handle it myself –'

The person who did, an agent who managed several properties, lived on the other side of the Gamaliya. It was another hot day and by the time Owen had reached him, his clothes were wet with perspiration. He was received again with courtesy and tea; and again given the run around.

'Well, of course, I had no idea what they wanted it for. A celebration of some sort, I believe they said. Too large for their own house so they wanted to hire a bigger one.'

'Do you have their names?'

The agent spread his hands regretfully.

'I'm afraid not,' he said.

That was unlikely, Owen remarked.

'They pay the money first,' the man said, smiling.

Owen got nowhere. He walked back to Bab-el-Khalk with Selim, dripping.

'The Gamaliya's a no-good place, effendi,' said Selim, commiserating. 'Now, over by the fish market, where I live —'

Owen stopped in his tracks.

'Selim,' he said, 'are you married?'

'Well, yes, effendi,' said Selim, taken aback. 'There's Leila, and there's Aisha, and there's —'

He began, however, to look troubled.

'Effendi,' he said hesitantly, 'I don't think they'd be good enough for you. Not yet. I mean, I'm trading up. In a bit, I'll divorce Aisha, and then I'll look out for someone a bit classier. In fact, I know a girl already who would do. She would just suit —'

'No, no, no, no!' said Owen hastily. 'Not that at all.'

He explained what he wanted.

Selim listened carefully.

'Well,' he said, 'Aisha's the one. She's a bit of a bitch, that's why I'm thinking of getting rid of her. Nag, nag, nag all the time, just come back late and you're in trouble. But she's got a good head on her. Mind you,' he looked worried, 'it could give her ideas, she would start getting above herself —'

'There would be money in it,' said Owen. 'For you.'

'Well, in that case —' said Selim, brightening. He thought it over. 'Yes,' he said, 'Aisha's definitely the one. She could say she was possessed by an evil spirit, all right. In fact, it wouldn't be too far from the truth . . .'

5

Garvin asked Owen if he would drop in on him before he went home. It was a request and courteous, so Owen knew that Garvin had found out that the Philipides business was about to be reopened.

He found him not sitting behind his desk, as was usually the case, but standing by the window, looking down through the shutters into the courtyard; as if he had just seen some donkeys there to which he took exception.

He was a big man, well over six feet in height and with huge broad shoulders. Despite twenty years of Egyptian sun, and Egyptian malaria, his face was fair and ruddy as if he had just arrived from English fields. The impression caught a truth about the man. Garvin came from one of the old English country families, no longer property own-ing but still country living. His father, a youngest son, had been a clergyman, but a clergyman of the 'squarson' sort, both squire and parson. Garvin had been brought up in the country and, though a university man (Cambridge), his pursuits were those of the country squire: riding, shooting and fishing. And, of course, hunting.

But there was another side to the man which the bluff exterior concealed. Garvin was no fool. He had spent two decades in the country and knew his job back to front. He knew it at all levels, too. He spoke Arabic like an Egyp-tian and was as familiar with the patois of the Alexandrian seafront underworld as he was with the slow rhythms of the fellahin in the fields around Cairo. Because of the time he had spent in the provinces before coming to the city, he was intimate with the background of family feuds and alliances which the fellahin carried with them when they migrated to the city. The Cairo poor were still villagers at heart; and Garvin knew them as he knew his own face in the mirror.

Yet he had been to Cambridge, too, and this gave him entry to an inner club from whose members the rulers of Egypt and India and, indeed, England were almost exclusively drawn. Mixing on equal terms with the British elite, inevitably he mixed, too, with the Egyptian elite. He knew the political preoccupations of both.

Garvin was, then, a formidable operator. He knew Egypt from top to bottom; and behind the frank, open face and the honest blue eyes was a political mind of no mean order. He played bridge regularly with the Consul-General and the Financial Secretary. Garvin was a great card player.

If there was a plot against him, the plotters would have their work cut out. The Administration would close ranks around Garvin in a way that Owen knew they would not close around him. He was not a member of the magic circle. He had not been to Cambridge. His father had died young and his family had been too poor to do other than secure him a commission in the army. He was, too, a Welshman; slightly suspect even in the army.

He was the magic circle's servant, no closer to them, in the end, than he was to the Khedive. But they would expect him to protect Garvin. Certain things did not need to be spoken. He knew what the job was that he was being told to do.

In fact, he did not expect that to put much of a strain on him. Garvin, for all his faults, was honest. This would be a trumped-up charge, if charge it came to. It would be a political manoeuvre. Garvin, in any case, probably was not so much the object as a means: a means of hitting at the British Administration itself.

Owen sighed. He could see himself being forced to take sides. It was a thing he did not like, something he tried to avoid. Usually he got round it by interpreting his loyalty as to Egypt as a whole. There was a sense, a very real sense, as a matter of fact, in which the Khedive and the British Administration together formed the Government of Egypt. His loyalty was to that mystic concept; very mystic, he sometimes felt.

There was, though, a less mystic consideration. In a complex political game the outcome might require sacrifices. He could not see the magic circle going so far as to be ready to sacrifice one of themselves. They would be far more likely to sacrifice someone else; say, him.

Owen thought he had better take up card playing.

Garvin turned to him.

'I gather you know the situation,' he said.

Owen nodded.

'In general terms,' he said.

Garvin came back to his desk.

'Well, you'll be raking over the details later,' he said. 'That'll be the job of the investigation. The question is, though, what's the procedure to be?'

'The Parquet will be responsible, presumably.'

The Parquet, or Department of Prosecutions of the Ministry of Justice, was responsible for carrying out all investigations. The police merely reported a crime. A lawyer from the Parquet was then at once assigned to it and he was thenceforth responsible for investigating the circumstances, compiling the evidence, taking a view, and then, if the view was in favour of prosecution, presenting the case, as in the French judicial system, which the Egyptian closely resembled, to the appropriate court.

'Yes,' said Garvin, 'but if they get that far it will go to the Mixed Courts.'

The Mixed Courts were a feature unique to the Egyptian judicial system. Where cases involved foreigners, they were heard not by the native courts of law but by a court on which sat judicial representatives from the foreigner's own native country as well as the Egyptian judges.

'That being so,' said Garvin, 'and, considering that one

of the people involved is a senior member of the British Administration – me – it would seem desirable that a representative of the British Administration was attached to the case from the outset. Then, if it came to prosecution, the case that was presented would have the support of both countries.'

'Quite,' said Owen. 'If it came to that. But will the Parquet agree?'

'You must be joking!' said Paul in the bar that evening. 'The most they'll agree to, with their arms twisted high up behind their backs and the army indicating that it's about to come out on manoeuvres, is to the attachment of an observer.'

'That'll do,' said Owen.

'It will have to,' said Paul. 'Though it's not at all the same thing. The observer just observes. He doesn't join in the presentation of the case. Nor in the decision as to whether the case is to be presented. He can stick his oar in when it actually comes to the court but only as a secondary witness. The Old Man's not happy about that but it's as much as we've been able to get.'

'Do they genuinely want a conviction?'

'Probably not. They almost certainly know there's nothing to convict. What they're looking for, I suspect, is the publicity of its coming to court. It makes the British look bad to the outside world and it makes them look good to their own supporters.'

'It won't make them look so good if the case is a real shambles.'

Paul smiled.

'We've already tried that,' he said. 'I tried to get them to appoint some real duds to carry out the investigation, the likes of Mohammed Isbi. Said how greatly we respected his judgement, how much he had our confidence. Any case presented by him would be sure to have our support.'

'Well?'

'They wouldn't wear it, of course. They're not that daft. They know he's as thick as a post.'

'So who have they appointed?'

'Their best and brightest. Mahmoud.'

Mahmoud el Zaki was one of Owen's oldest friends. The two were actually very much alike, young men on the rise. They had met on one of Owen's earliest cases, which had turned out to be one of Mahmoud's first cases, too, and since then their careers had kept a parallel course. They were both self-sufficient, not exactly loners – Owen was quite gregarious – but standing a little apart from their fellows.

They were both to a certain extent outsiders: Owen because he stood outside the charmed circle of those who had been to public school and the ancient universities, and because of the ambiguity of the post of Mamur Zapt, responsible to the Egyptian and British Administrations; Mahmoud because he, too, was not by birth a member of the Egyptian elite. His father, a first generation graduate and, like Mahmoud himself, a lawyer, had died young while establishing a position and Mahmoud had inherited both the family's expectations and its lack of wealth and social connections. He had had to work hard to rise, to do it all himself. There was quite a lot in common between him and the Welsh grammar school boy from an impoverished Anglican family; not least a tendency to define for oneself a social identity by siding with the suppressed Nationalist opposition.

Mahmoud was in fact formally a member of the new Nationalist Party, which did him no harm in the Parquet but which left him politically and socially uneasy when it came to encounters with representatives of the Egyptian elite. He was, for example, completely at sea when it came to talking to Zeinab. This was, however, only partly because she was the daughter of a Pasha. Like most educated young Egyptians, Mahmoud had hardly ever met a respectable young woman and did not know exactly how one should behave. Besides, he wasn't completely sure that Zeinab *was* respectable and when they met usually finished up looking down between her feet with embarrassment.

He and Owen were sufficiently close for Owen to be able to ring him up and say: 'Hey, about this Garvin business; can we have a talk?'

'Yes, yes!' cried Mahmoud at once. 'Come right over!' Then he thought again. 'Um, well, perhaps you'd better not. Not here, at any rate.'

'Lunch? Marsali's?'

'Yes, yes!' said Mahmoud, eager to make amends. 'Today! This afternoon!'

'Right, then. One o'clock.'

One o'clock found him in a little street just off the Mouski, far enough down to be away from the clangs of the trams in the Ataba-el-Khadra, not so far down as to be completely within the purview of the old part of the city where the cafés tended to be pavement ones and you squatted on your haunches around a large tray on the ground and dipped your bread in; all very well, but not good for weighty conversation.

Mahmoud jumped up at his approach and threw his arms around him, Arab style.

'It's been so long!' he said enthusiastically (about a week). 'What have you been doing?'

'As little as possible,' said Owen.

'I know! The heat! It's been impossible in the courts. Two witnesses collapsed yesterday. Mustapha Kamil' – one of the senior judges – 'said he'd have to bring the sessions to an end early if things didn't improve. I'd be against that, though,' added Mahmoud seriously. 'It would merely add to the backlog. We're six months behind as it is.'

Mahmoud was a strong believer in hard work and efficiency. He and Garvin were birds of a feather.

'It can't be long before the sessions end anyway, can it?'

'Two weeks. But really, there's so much still to get through, we ought to extend it.'

'That would be popular!'

He sometimes thought Mahmoud was a bit unyielding.

A broad smile spread over Mahmoud's face, relaxing the intensity.

'It doesn't stand a chance!' he said.

The waiter took their orders.

'At any rate,' said Mahmoud, 'it will give us plenty of time to settle the Garvin *affaire*.'

'Is it the Garvin affair?' asked Owen. 'Or is it the Philipides affair?'

Mahmoud shrugged.

'It's the corruption affair. That's the only way to look at it. We don't make any judgements until we've had another look at the evidence.'

'Where are you going to start?'

'With the original sub-inspector. That's ultimately where the charges came from. His name's Bakri.'

'Mind if I sit in?'

'Not at all.' Mahmoud hesitated. 'But as a friend,' he said, 'a colleague. Not as an official observer.'

'I thought that had been agreed?'

'It has and it hasn't. What's been agreed is that your status must be informal. But the people making the agreement were not – well, they were politicians, not lawyers. "Observer" expressed what they thought they meant. But there is no provision under the legal system for an observer. In a case like this I think it's important to keep to the letter of the law. So, no observers. But as a friend and colleague you are most welcome.'

'Doesn't it amount to the same thing?'

'In practice, with you, yes. But the judicial system must be free, and be seen to be free, from political interference. It's a question,' said Mahmoud firmly but, looking at Owen, a little anxiously, 'of principle.'

Mahmoud was strong on principles.

'There must be no British finger in the scales,' he said determinedly.

Abdul Bakri was still a sub-inspector.

'No, it didn't go through,' he said. 'Then or later. When you're involved in something like this, you know, they don't forget. People don't like it.'

'Those who were involved at the time may not have liked it,' said Mahmoud. 'But they're all gone, surely?'

'No one likes it,' said Abdul Bakri dispiritedly. 'When you've done it once, whoever's your boss after that thinks you're going to do it again.'

'It will only worry them if they've got something to hide.'

'We've all got something to hide,' said Abdul Bakri. 'Everyone bends the rules at some time.'

Mahmoud, who never bent the rules, was shocked into silence for a moment.

'It's your mates, too,' Abdul Bakri went on. 'They don't like it.'

'They're the ones who benefited!'

'Well, I don't know about that.'

'They didn't like having to pay for promotion, surely?'

'Well, at least you knew where you were. Forty pounds would get you an inspectorship. All you had to do was to save up. Cost you a bit, of course, but then you wouldn't want everybody becoming an inspector. The point is, if you could find the money, you were all right. There was none of this funny business of people deciding how good you are. You see, that sort of thing makes it really chancey. You might have served in the force for twenty years and then someone comes along and says: "No, you can't be an inspector because you're too lazy" or not clever enough. Now, I don't call that fair at all. Whereas if all you had to do was find the money, it couldn't go wrong, could it?'

'I see,' said Mahmoud. 'And you're still a sub-inspector.'

'That's right,' said Abdul Bakri, aggrieved. 'Spoiled my

chance of promotion, that's what he did, Garvin effendi!'

'You could have said nothing,' Mahmoud pointed out.

'Fat chance of that!' said Abdul Bakri. 'He had me in his office and he said: "Forty pounds, Abdul Bakri? What's that for?" Well, I tried to put him off, but he said: "It wouldn't be, by any chance, to purchase an inspectorship, would it?" Well, after that . . . "I know all about it," he said. "So you'd better just tell me." There wasn't much I could do, was there? He had me.'

'Did he remind you of your rights?'

'Rights?' said Abdul Bakri incredulously. 'Look, let me tell you, a sub-inspector's got no rights. Not in the police force, he hasn't.'

'Attempted bribery is an offence,' said Mahmoud severely.

'Don't I know it! That's just what Garvin effendi said. He said, "It's prison for you, my lad, if you don't do what I say." I said, "What about the money?" He said, "You've had that." Well, I mean, forty pounds is a lot of money, it was all I had. It wasn't really mine, either. I mean, it was Leila's jewellery and she hadn't been too pleased in the first place. If it had gone for good, well, she'd have killed me. Prison, I didn't mind; well, at least you've got food and a roof over your head, haven't you, but to have Leila forever on my back — "Well, all right, effendi," I said, "I'll do what you want!"'

'And what did Garvin effendi want?'

'He said, "Who have you been dealing with? Have you been talking to Philipides direct?" And I said, No, it had all been done through Philipides's orderly, Hassan. So he said: "Right then, you tell Hassan that you're a bit worried about going on with it because you've heard that Garvin effendi knows all about it." "Effendi," I said, "have you got it right? The first thing Hassan will do will be to tell Philipides." "That's right!" said Garvin effendi, and gave that little smile of his. Anyway, I did what he told me and Hassan went as white as a sheet and rushed off. The next day, he was back with the forty pounds, well, thirty-nine pounds, in fact, and said, "Here you are, we don't want to know any more about it."'

'Thirty-nine pounds?'

'That bastard, Hassan, was taking his cut. Got his fingers burnt that time, though, I can tell you. Garvin effendi said, "You go to Hassan and tell him you want all the money or else there'll be trouble. And tell him he's got to bring it to you at the police station tomorrow morning." Well, I did, and Hassan didn't like it, but he brought the money. But what he didn't know was that Garvin effendi had got two men in the next room listening in. So he had him cold,' said Abdul Bakri, 'and after that the thing just rolled.'

'Are we going to talk to Hassan?' asked Owen, as they walked back.

'We can't.'

'Why not?'

'Because he disappeared.'

'Fearing the worst?'

'Or because of intimidation.'

'Yes,' said Owen, 'I gather there was a lot of that going on.'

'On both sides,' said Mahmoud, 'judging by Abdul Bakri's account.'

'Well, I had to say something. So I said something came over me at the full moon. I thought my husband was a pig and wanted to engage in unnatural practices with me. "What sort of practices?" she said.'

'I don't think we need go into this,' said Selim uneasily.

His wife, however, enjoying the opportunity, thought otherwise; and did with relish.

'And then I said I thought he was an ox,' she said happily. 'Not from the point of view of getting on with his work uncomplainingly but because of his stupidity –'

'Look, Aisha,' Selim began.

'I complained how often my husband beat me. Because

of the times when I was possessed, that is. And then I asked her if she knew of an Aalima who could cast out the spirit from me. "It sounds as if your husband is the one who needs to see her," she said. "No, no," I said, "my husband is kind and patient and thoughtful and generous, hard-working and considerate –"'

'Aisha, if you don't – !'

Over the heavy veil the big eyes looked at Owen demurely.

'"I am the one possessed", I said. "That I could ever think of him otherwise!" "Well," she said, "I've got a cousin in the Gamaliya and she knows an Aalima", so we went to the cousin and she said she would speak to the Aalima. And the Aalima agreed to see me. "What is your trouble?" she asked. And I said, "Every full moon I think my husband is a pig." "A pig?" she said. "Yes," I said, "a pig."'

'Aisha –'

'"Why is that?" she asked. "Because he wishes to engage in unnatural practices with me. Or, at least, that's what I imagine. When I'm possessed."'

'Aisha –'

'"What sort of unnatural practices –?"'

'All right, all right,' Owen broke in. 'We've got that bit.'

'You wait till you get home!' said Selim.

'None of that!' said Owen. 'Or you don't get paid.'

'Yes, but, effendi –'

'Did the Aalima agree?'

'Well, she said she'd just held a Zzarr and ordinarily she wouldn't have another one for several months. However, it had raised a lot of interest in the neighbourhood and since it had been held, quite a few women had come forward, so that she thought that perhaps she'd better hold another one as otherwise it wouldn't be fair –'

'Did she give you a date?'

'Next week sometime. She'll let me know. I'll need time to prepare, you see.'

'Prepare?'

'I have to purify myself. No sex beforehand and none for a month afterwards – '

'A month!' said Selim, aghast.

'At least. You'll just have to ask Leila.'

'It's the wrong time of the month for her.'

'Oh dear,' said Aisha.

The city drooped in the heat. From about mid-morning the streets were deserted. Even the Ataba-el-Khadra, the square where most of Cairo's tram routes terminated, and which was normally bustling with people, seemed empty. The drivers of the trams clanged their bells half-heartedly, and departed half empty. No one wished to travel if they could avoid it.

The tourist season was at an end now and outside the big hotels the ranks were full of arabeahs. Their drivers dozed in the shade beneath their vehicles and did not even bother to look for custom. The donkey boys below the hotel terraces played endless games with sticks and white stones. Their donkeys slept on their feet. Even in sleep their tails twitched continuously against the flies.

During the season, the street in front of the main European hotels was crowded with hawkers selling everything from souvenirs of the tombs to dirty postcards. Now all the hawkers had gone, as had the tumblers, and acrobats, the musicians and the people with performing monkeys. Only a solitary, blind snake charmer remained. Hearing Owen approach, he began to play on his flute. The snake rose slowly from its basket.

Did snakes have ears? Owen wondered. He couldn't remember ever having noticed any. He couldn't see any on this one, either. Perhaps they were sunk in or something? He would have liked to have looked more closely, but then again, he wasn't sure he wanted to look too closely. His friend the snake catcher had said they always removed the poison fangs before selling them on but Owen didn't want to be the first to find an exception.

'Have they got ears?' he asked the snake charmer.

The charmer stopped in mid-trill.

'Ears?' he said incredulously. 'Of course not!'

'Well, then, how do they hear the music?'

'Look, are you trying to catch me out?' said the snake charmer angrily, blaring a short blast on his flute.

The snake's head stopped its rhythmic swinging and hung in the air. It certainly seemed to be responding to the music; but perhaps there was some other cue it was responding to? The old man's swaying, for instance? Or perhaps vibration was picked up in a different way.

The charmer stopped playing and the snake returned to its basket. The old man replaced the lid crossly and stumped away. Owen would have liked to have asked him more questions but this was clearly not the occasion. He would have to ask someone else. His own snake catcher, for instance. Or perhaps that girl.

He had been thinking about the snakes as he had been walking along. Because that was the bit that needed explanation. He could understand what had happened at the Zzarr. They hadn't wanted McPhee to see the ceremony so they had drugged him. But why put him in the cistern with the snakes? Were snakes something to do with the Zzarr? Had some religious significance, perhaps?

There was only one way to find out. He wasn't a McPhee, interested in ceremony for its own sake, nor did he wish to do a McPhee, poke his nose in where he wasn't wanted. But he was beginning to feel that a lot of the questions he was asking could only be answered by knowing more about what went on at a Zzarr and the best way of finding out was to go to one.

He could treat it as a reconstruction of the crime, perhaps. Mahmoud, with his background in French law, would like that. The Parquet, steeped in the French judicial system and trained to apply French criminal procedures, were keen on reconstructions. He was not sure, though, that simply going to a Zzarr would come into that category.

And ought he to be wasting his time on that sort of

thing, anyway? Oughtn't he to be concentrating on the Mahmoud investigation? But the pace in that was set by Mahmoud and he was having to juggle the time he spent on that against the demands of the other things on his plate. Owen reminded himself that he was just an observer; if that.

No, he had to leave the initiative to Mahmoud. The McPhee business on the other hand was clearly his responsibility and he ought to get on with it. Not because of McPhee himself – they might all be having a peaceful time if it had not been for that blockhead – but because of the danger of it spilling over into communal violence. And was there someone behind it all? It did look a bit like it.

He decided to go and see the witch.

6

She was not exactly pleased to see him.

He had left it, deliberately, as late as he could so that she would not have time to cancel the Zzarr or rearrange it in another place. The outer courtyard was already full of people and there were lamps inside the house. Musicians were tuning up.

The house was not the one she had used before but very like it. There was both an outer courtyard and an inner one. The men were congregated in the outer courtyard and stopped him when he tried to pass through to the inner one.

'Can't do that,' they said. 'Women only.'

'I wish to speak to the Aalima.'

'She won't see you.'

'I think she will. Tell her it's the Mamur Zapt.'

There was a sudden hush.

'All right,' said someone at last, 'but she won't like it. There could be trouble.'

'There'll be trouble all right,' said Selim, big and bulky behind Owen, 'if you don't do what the Mamur Zapt says.'

'I come in peace,' said Owen.

One of the men called through into the inner courtyard and spoke to a woman there.

While he was waiting for the Aalima, Owen glanced around him. There were lighted braziers both in the outer courtyard and the inner one and he could smell coffee in both. The men were standing around chatting animatedly. There was something of a party atmosphere.

'Your wife in there?' said Owen conversationally to a man near him.

'Daughter. My wife can't go tonight – her sister's having a baby – but she said Khadiya had to go. Don't believe in this sort of thing myself.'

'Can't do any harm,' said another man.

'Can't it? My wife comes home half-crazed.'

'She gets over it, though, doesn't she?'

'Yes, but what's been going on while she has been out of her mind? That's what I'd like to know. You don't know what they get up to.'

'There aren't any men there, though, are there?' said Selim wistfully.

'You don't always need men.'

'No?'

Through the arch Owen could see white forms approaching. He moved to meet them.

'Who is it who wishes to speak with me?' said the Aalima.

'Greetings, Mother,' said Owen politely. 'May we step aside for a moment?'

Just beyond the arch a little room gave off the courtyard. He had time only to see that the inner yard was full of women and children in white gowns. The smell of incense hung in the air and on the other side of the ring of firelight cast by a brazier he thought he saw animals stirring restlessly.

The Aalima led Owen into the room and then turned towards him. She had a large white cowl over her head but was unveiled and there was just enough light from the single oil lamp for him to see her face.

'Ya salaam!' he said in surprise. He had expected to see an old crone. This woman was at the most in her thirties and had a handsome, classical face.

'What is it you want?' she said impatiently. 'I do nothing wrong.'

'I'm sure not. Nevertheless, at the last Zzarr you held, wrong things were done.'

'The Bimbashi? That was nothing to do with me.'

'I wasn't thinking just of the Bimbashi. I was thinking of the Copts.'

'That was nothing to do with me, either. Or with the Zzarr.'

'You may be right,' said Owen. 'Nevertheless, it was at the Zzarr that something happened to the Bimbashi.'

'If you have questions to ask,' said the Aalima, 'you must put them another time. The Zzarr is about to begin.'

'You carry on,' said Owen. 'I'll wait.'

'You can't wait here,' said the Aalima. 'This is for women only.'

'I won't interfere.'

'You cannot stay,' said the woman angrily. 'Please go!'

'I'll wait.'

A *mastaba*, a long stone bench, ran along one side of the room. He sat down.

The woman bit her lip.

'I'll answer your questions tomorrow,' she said.

'Ah,' said Owen, 'but will you be here tomorrow?'

'I will tell you where I live.'

'Tell me,' said Owen, 'and I will send a man to make sure that that is indeed where you live.'

'I live on the other side of the Gamaliya,' she protested.

'We can wait. Or you could begin.'

She stood there for a moment. Then her foot began to tap angrily.

'Why are you here?' she burst out furiously. 'Why was the Bimbashi here?'

'The Bimbashi was lured here,' said Owen. 'I want to find out why.'

'That was nothing to do with me! You cannot stay here!'

Owen settled himself on the *mastaba*. The Aalima then rushed from the room. Out in the courtyard, women's voices began to chatter urgently.

'Are you all right, effendi?' called Selim's voice.

Owen got up from the *mastaba* and went to the door.

'Yes, thanks,' he called back. Then, seeing Selim standing in the arch, he walked over to him.

'I'm just waiting to see if she bites,' he said.

'Bites?' said Selim, intrigued. 'Oh, bites. There'll be plenty of that later.'

Owen thought Selim might be misunderstanding him. However, the constable pointed beyond the brazier to where the animals were stirring. He could see now that one of them was a large ram.

'Sacrifice?' he said. 'Or a feast?'

'Both,' said Selim. 'The Aalima does pretty well out of it. She gets half of it, you know.'

'She doesn't *eat* half, surely?'

'No, no. She sells it. Makes a pretty piastre. What with that and the fee everyone pays.'

'She wouldn't want to miss out on it, would she?' said Owen thoughtfully.

'Hello, my lovely!' said Selim to one of the white forms. A group of gowns rushed up and pushed him indignantly into the arch.

Owen returned to the *mastaba*.

After about a quarter of an hour the Aalima appeared.

'The Zzarr is off!' she said fiercely. 'I have asked my women. They say they cannot begin if a man is present.'

She folded her arms firmly. Owen knew suddenly whom she reminded him of. Not for her beauty but for her manner; the Scottish Matron at the Cairo Hospital.

'I do not wish to interfere,' he said mildly. 'I will stay in this room if you like. That hardly counts as being present, surely?'

'The Zzarr is off!' said the Aalima, with a triumphant smile.

Owen shrugged.

'Very well, then,' he said, rising to his feet. 'Tell them to return the animals.'

The Aalima's smile faded.

'What happens to the animals is no business of yours!' she snapped.

'I'll tell them,' said Owen, as he went out. 'Selim!'

'Wait! Wait!'

'I could sit here,' Owen offered. 'It wouldn't really count.'

The Aalima hesitated.

'You must not look,' she said, weakening.

Owen pointed to the wall.

'If I looked,' he said, 'could I see?'

The Aalima made up her mind.

'Very well. You can stay. But if you set one foot outside this room,' she said coldly, 'the Zzarr stops.'

As soon as she had gone, Owen extinguished the lamp. It took a short while for his eyes to get used to the darkness but when they did, he found he could see quite well. Moonlight came in through the open door and lit up the white wall opposite him. He took care to stay in the shadow.

After a moment or two, he heard people outside.

'He has put the light out,' someone said.

There was a muttered consultation.

'Are you still there?' a woman's voice called out.

'Of course,' said Owen.

'Why have you put the light out?'

'Out of respect.'

More consultation.

'There's no need to do that,' someone said.

'That's all right,' said Owen.

The consultation became agitated.

'We are going to shut the door,' a voice called out.

'Please don't do that. It's so hot in here.'

He heard the discussion.

'It's a trick!'

'Yes, but it *is* hot in there.'

'We must ask the Aalima,' said someone after a while.

'It's too late,' said someone. 'It's beginning.'

Across the courtyard, in the main building, a timbrel was starting uncertainly.

'I promise I won't come out.'

Dubertas began to catch the rhythm.

'Very well, then. But mind you don't! We are putting people to watch!'

'That is not necessary. But if you wish to –'

There was a mighty clash of cymbals and then all the instruments were playing together. A voice joined in, wavering, hanging, posing a question or an invitation. Another voice answered.

The people outside lingered irresolutely, then went away. Someone else came up and sat down just outside the door. The guard had been posted. It was, however, a very small one. About twelve years old, Owen judged.

There were a lot of children in the courtyard, many of them dressed in white gowns like the Aalima's companions. As the music caught hold, they began to dance.

Owen watched for a little while and then moved round the room until he could see out of the doorway. The main activity was going on in a room opposite. It was a long room, probably the *mandar'ah*, or reception room, which ran the whole length of one side of the inner courtyard. The music was coming from one end, where there was a dais, on which the performers sat. If they were men there would be a screen between them and the rest of the hall.

The music deepened and other voices joined in, passing the question or invitation from one to another until suddenly they all began to sing together. Owen could still not tell whether they were men or women. Nor could he quite make out the words although some of them seemed familiar. But what language?

There was movement on the other end of the *mandar'ah*. He could see the Aalima standing beside what looked like a little table. Round her a ring of white-gowned women was forming. They were holding hands, or holding on to something; a rope, perhaps. The ring began to spin.

Outside in the courtyard little rings of children began

to spin also. It was like 'Ring-a-ring of roses' only speeded up.

He suddenly caught something move just outside the door and hastily slid back on to the *mastaba*. A figure entered.

'No light?' said a voice he thought he had heard before.

'Out of respect,' said Owen.

'Oh yes!' said the voice ironically. He was sure now he had heard it before.

The figure stooped. It was holding something out to him.

'Take and drink,' said the voice.

'Thank you,' said Owen. He tipped the bowl towards him and let the liquid touch his lips. It was hot and spicy. As far as he could tell, there was no drug in it. This time.

That other time, McPhee had been sitting out in the courtyard. They had put a chair just beneath the windows. He had been so close, he had told Owen, that he had been intoxicated by the music.

The music continued, the circles, both inside the house and out in the courtyard, continued to spin. The next time the woman came with the bowl, Owen could see her more clearly.

'You!' he said in surprise.

'Why not?' said the snake-catcher's daughter.

He held the bowl back for a moment after drinking.

'Do you always do this?' he asked. 'Take the bowl round at the Zzarr?'

'We all have our parts to play,' she said ambiguously.

He relinquished the bowl.

'You are a woman of many parts,' he said.

He saw the smile in the moonlight. When he had seen her before, beside the snake cistern, he had been too busy to notice her face. It was a rather pretty one. He realized suddenly that none of the women this evening were wearing veils. Some of the more modest ones had pulled their hoods forward over their faces. The Aalima and her acolytes, however, were having none of such half measures.

The hoods were thrown back well behind the neck. Girls among girls, Owen supposed.

The snake-catcher's daughter seemed disposed to linger.

'I take the bowl round,' she said, 'because I can't be one of those inside.'

'Oh? Why not?'

'I'm not clean.'

He did not understand. Then he remembered what Selim's wife had said.

'You haven't been purified?'

'I can't be.'

'How's that?'

'I haven't been cut.' Seeing that Owen was at a loss, she explained: 'When you're a girl, they cut you. They pare it back. Afterwards, they sew you.'

'Oh,' said Owen, understanding at last. 'Circumcision?'

'That's right. Only my father wouldn't let them do it to me. He said the snakes would notice.'

Owen wondered *how* the snakes would notice.

'The smell,' she said.

'Do you mind?' he asked.

'Not being done? I haven't up till now,' she said. 'But now, sometimes, I wonder. I cannot be a woman, you see,' she explained, 'until that is done. Although –' she shot a glance in the direction of the house – 'I'm more of a woman than some of those in there, I can tell you!'

'Some would say,' said Owen carefully, 'that there are advantages in not having been cut.'

'Really?' she said.

He had taken care not to drink from the bowl. He had just let the liquid touch his lips. He had also put a finger in, and when she had gone he smelt the finger and tasted with his tongue. Still, as far as he could judge, no drug.

'How's it going, effendi!' said a well-known voice right beside him.

He jumped.

'Selim! Christ, what are you doing here? They've got a guard outside.'

'Just a kid. And gone off to join the dancing, anyway.'
Selim went to the door and peered out. 'Wow, effendi!
How about that?'

The rhythm of the music had risen to fever pitch. The
women inside had arched their bodies back, still holding
hands, so that they touched the ground only with their
heels and their heads, continuing to writhe, however, to
the rhythm.

'Yow!' said Selim. 'Wow!'

The music came suddenly to a stop with a violent clash
of cymbals. The exhausted women sank to the ground.
All over the courtyard similar rings were collapsing.

'You'd better get back,' said Owen.

'Effendi,' said Selim, 'there's something I've been wanting to ask you.'

'Yes?'

'Can I transfer to your service? Constable's all very well
but it's nothing like this!'

'Get off back!' snapped Owen. 'Quick!'

Only just in time, for the snake-catcher's daughter reappeared with the bowl.

'What's your name?' asked Owen, taking it from her.

'Jalila.'

'Why don't you sit down, Jalila? There seems a bit of a
break in proceedings.'

'This is when they need the drink,' she said, but she sat
down; on the floor, however.

'Is it a special drink?' he asked.

'It keeps them going.'

It was drugged, then. He dipped his finger in and held
it to his tongue. It seemed subtly different. But perhaps
that was just from having been told. And was he being
given the same drink as the others?

'They will be thirsty,' he said, 'after all that dancing.'

'They go on all night,' she said. 'It's only just started.'

'They dance the whole time?'

'Until the sacrifices.'

'They must be exhausted!'

'That's why the men are here,' she said. 'To carry them home.'

'Have you a man here?'

She smiled.

'I'm not dancing,' she said.

The next time she came the taste of the drink was stronger and deeper. He thought that perhaps there were two drugs, one for the dancers, to keep them going, the other the one that McPhee had taken. Perhaps they had not put that one in yet. Perhaps they would not put it in at all tonight, knowing that he was the Mamur Zapt and guessing that he would be forewarned. He would go on tasting, not drinking; although, as a matter of fact, he felt he could really do with a drink, a long, iced, cool one.

The music had started again and the dancing was picking up.

'No drinking either?' he said to Jalila.

She shook her head.

'I just carry the bowl,' she said.

'Someone, at least, has to know what they're doing?'

She seemed slightly puzzled.

'The Aalima knows what she's doing,' she said.

The Aalima, from what he saw between Jalila's visits, was doing very little dancing herself. She seemed content to preside, occasionally moving to the centre of the ring and letting them spin round her, occasionally stepping to the table and holding something up. He could see fruit, cakes and flowers on the table, together with a few pots, one of which she raised from time to time.

It was different this time. He could tell that before it touched his lips. The fumes were heady. Owen had a particularly acute sense of smell and knew they were different. They reached up into his head and hung there. He tried to identify them but could not.

He wanted her to leave quickly so that he could breathe heavily to clear his head but she put the bowl to one side and squatted amicably on the floor.

'How often does she hold a Zzarr?' he asked.

Jalila smiled.

'As often as she can,' she said. 'It pays her.'

'Half the meat?'

'And the fees. Everyone who comes, pays a fee. And then the ones who are possessed, they pay a lot.'

'I can understand that,' said Owen. 'But why do the others pay?'

Jalila shrugged.

'They all like it,' she said. 'It's a bit of fun. There's not much going on round here, after all. Not for women.'

'The Aalima wants it, women want it. I suppose the only thing that stops her having them all the time is the supply of people possessed by spirits.'

'There are always plenty of those,' said Jalila with a touch of scorn.

'You don't think they're really possessed?'

A loud blast of the dubertas and timbrels recalled Jalila to her duties. She stood up, a trifle regretfully.

'We've all got a bit of the devil in us,' she said.

He handed the bowl back to her. The move shot fresh fumes into the air.

'It's a long night for you in here,' Jalila said.

Owen wondered if this was an invitation.

'I'll try not to fall asleep,' he said.

Jalila laughed.

Like a girls' party, he thought. In the courtyard the children danced. It was more crowded now and there were women among them. He could see by the taller, fuller forms. There was girlish laughter, the occasional high-pitched giggle.

Selim reappeared.

'Hello!' he said, sniffing. 'What's this?'

'What sent the Bimbashi to sleep.'

'Those bitches!'

'They don't want me to see.'

'I should think not! The way they dance!'

'Is Aisha dancing too?'

'Like that? I hope not. I wouldn't have thought she had it in her. Do you think she has it in her?' he asked Owen in worried tones.

'We've all got a bit of the devil in us,' said Owen.

He wondered how Selim's wife was faring. He hoped she was all right. What if the supposedly possessed were given special treatment, some special drug of their own? He ought to have thought of that earlier.

'Smells a bit ripe in here,' said Selim.

'Yes,' said Owen, thinking.

After Selim had gone, he sat back slumped against the wall and did not move when Jalila next came in. He felt her cool hand touch his face. It hesitated, as if she were puzzled. Then she went out again.

A little later, doors were closed over the arch which separated the inner courtyard from the outer. There was a sudden bleating of animals.

Owen crept to the door.

In the courtyard now everything was still. The Aalima appeared at the door holding what seemed to be a huge basin. The animals were led up to her. There was a huge black ram and then two young white ones stained red with henna. Behind them were other animals, ganders, doves, rabbits. A man was standing there, blind, Owen judged, from his white eyes. He held a long knife and as each animal was led up, he slit its throat and held it over the Aalima's basin.

The Aalima took the basin and went back indoors. Owen saw her appear at the other end of the *mandar'ah*. She went into the middle of the ring of women, dipped her arms suddenly in the basin and then threw blood all over them. The women screamed, then pressed forward, dipped their own arms in the basin, then threw.

The music burst out in a savage frenzy. The women began to writhe, twisting from side to side, leaning back as before but now dancing round on their heels with their heads up and their hair dangling out behind them. As they whirled, the Aalima continued to throw blood. The white gowns were all bespotted with red now, blood was on the women's faces, in their hair. Girls' party?

McPhee was disappointed afterwards.

'But, Owen,' he complained, 'didn't you *see*?'

'Well, of course I did,' said Owen defensively, 'but –'

'The vestments? You must have noticed alb, amice and girdle?'

'Alb?'

'The long white gown.'

'Amice?'

'A square of white linen. Worn formerly on the head. Now on the shoulders.'

'She wore a sort of hood. That it?'

'Yes. And did you notice – I thought it was very significant – that when she served at the altar –'

'Altar? Oh, that table, you mean.'

'Really, Owen!' said McPhee severely. 'I thought you told me that your father was a minister in the Church of England?'

'Yes, but, well, it's not the same, is it? I mean, an altar is something you find in church –'

'Ah! But that's it, you see. For them it was the same thing as being in a church. The offerings –'

'The animals, you mean? That old ram –?'

'Think of Abraham. Animals came before money, you know.'

'It seemed pretty gory to me.'

'But that's just what I've been saying! Religious elements – I do wish you'd observed it more closely, Owen. I was particularly anxious that you confirmed my perception that when she was engaged on ceremonies at the altar she *raised* her amice, raised it above her head; I mean, that's *terribly* significant: Capuchin, would you say, or Dominican?'

'Yes, but the gore –'

'Religious *elements*, Owen, but *pre*-Christian at the core.

Cultic influence, I am sure. Baal, perhaps? Or perhaps Tammuz?'

'Well, I couldn't say, offhand –'

'Didn't you ask her anything?'

'We didn't have a lot of time,' said Owen feebly. 'She said she'd answer my questions tomorrow.'

'Well, mind you ask her that. Even so, Owen, a missed opportunity!' McPhee shook his head sadly. 'A missed opportunity!'

'I spoke to Jalila.'

'Jalila?'

'She's the one with the bowl.'

'Charming girl, charming. But it's a pity you didn't speak to one of the acolytes.'

'Acolytes?'

'Deaconesses, I call them. The ones with the maniples.'

'Oh!'

'I did ask Jalila – Jalila you said her name was? – about them. I asked her if they were virgins.'

'And what did she say?'

'"Virgins born, effendi."' McPhee frowned. 'But that, of course, is not quite answering my question.'

'Well, I'll ask it,' said Owen, 'if I get an opportunity.'

'And the initiates.'

'What about the initiates?'

'Ask if they were virgins, too.'

'I don't think I can go around asking everybody if they're a virgin.'

'Well, perhaps not,' said McPhee, disappointed. 'Only it would be so interesting to know.'

'It certainly would,' said Owen.

Selim was disappointed too.

'They shut the gate,' he complained. 'Just when it was getting interesting.'

'You missed the best part,' said Aisha.

'There's luck for you!' said Selim, crestfallen. 'I was hoping that the next time I went round –'

'Next time?' said Owen.

'Well, that first time when I went to you, I didn't go straight to you, if you know what I mean –'

'We know what you mean,' said Aisha.

'I thought there might be trouble later on, so I took a look around –'

'Look?' said Aisha.

'Well, all right, maybe a touch too, here and there.'

'Someone gave me a touch,' said Aisha.

'You?' said Selim, eyes starting out of his head. 'You?'

'Of course it might have been someone else,' said Aisha, eyes smiling meekly over her veil.

7

'Is that Mustapha?'

  'Speaking.'

'The line is bad. I wasn't sure it was you.'

'The line is always bad. It is best not to use it.'

'I had to use it. Mustapha, I must warn you. They have seized Hassan.'

  'So?'

'He is being questioned.'

'What can he say?'

'He can tell them things that lead to us.'

'Hassan is too clever to do that. And if he did, we could always deny them.'

'Mustapha, I'm afraid you don't understand. Abdul Bakri has talked. They know he has given money to Hassan. It will lead to us.'

'"They". "They". Who are "They"?'

'Garvin. Mustapha, he has had Hassan in —'

'Garvin is "he", not "they". Who are the others?'

'Mustapha —'

'Not Wainwright Pasha, I take it? No? The Consul-General, then? Is it someone around the Consul-General?'

'I — I do not think so, Mustapha. I do not know. Mustapha, I —'

'But this is important. Please. Are there others? Or is it just Garvin?'

'Perhaps it is just Garvin.'

  'Ah!'

'But, Mustapha, it does not make any difference. He will soon tell others.'

'It makes a lot of difference. I need to know what is behind this. If it is just Garvin, well, I will go to Wainwright Pasha at once and knock this *canard* on the head. People are always saying things against us. That is the nature of our job. It has happened before, it will happen again.'

'But, Mustapha, this is not anyone saying this, it is Garvin.'

'One unsupported man, new to Cairo, credulous. What does he know about our world? People tell us things, we listen, because that is the nature of our work, but we do not always believe them. They offer us money and sometimes we take it, because that, too, is the nature of our work, but our intention may be different from theirs. Wainwright Pasha knows all this but Garvin, what does he know? A simple policeman from Alexandria!'

'Mustapha, I do not think he is that simple.'

'It is the nature of his work that is simple. Compared with ours.'

'Mustapha, I still worry –'

'And I worry, too. But not for the same reason as you. If things are as you say they are, then I do not worry. It is if there are things behind them that I worry.'

'I hope you are right, Mustapha . . . But, please, what shall I do?'

'Do not phone me again, that is the first. The second is: carry on with your work and do not fear. But the third is: let me know the moment you think it is they and not he that we have against us.'

'An open-and-shut case, I would have thought,' said Owen, laying the transcript back on the table. Police office ink faded quickly in the light and heat of Egypt and the writing was already brown, although it had been written only five years before. 'It's a virtual confession, surely.'

Mahmoud picked the transcript up and looked at it again.

'There are problems about using this kind of evidence in court,' he said. 'Were the words accurately recorded? Were they recorded at the time? Have the speakers been correctly identified?'

'You've got the sworn statements of the recorders here,' said Owen, tapping a folder which lay before him on Mahmoud's desk. 'Signed, dated, witnessed. They were people who knew the voices, too.'

'Oh yes,' said Mahmoud. 'Garvin had it all worked out.'

'Well, then –'

'But shall we see what Philipides says?'

Philipides was thin, almost painfully so. The prison report spoke of ulcers. Owen judged he was a worrying man. The small mouth beneath the neat moustache occasionally twitched involuntarily.

He still denied the charges. Not so much the facts as their interpretation. Yes, his orderly, Hassan, had approached Sub-Inspector Abdul Bakri and solicited money in return for a promise of promotion; but this was merely part of a carefully planned, and officially inspired, attempt to probe allegations of corruption in the Cairo Police Force. As Mustapha Mir, the Mamur Zapt of the time, would confirm.

The offer of promotion was not, then, genuine? Mahmoud asked. Certainly not; and the money would have been returned, with a severe warning.

But, surely, offering money – as well as accepting money – was a grave offence and should have resulted in something more serious than a warning?

'An official warning,' said Philipides. 'It would remain on his file.'

'Even so –'

'Ah, yes,' said Philipides, 'but corruption was so widespread – one could almost say it was the fashion of the country – that to come down heavily on a minor individual would have been manifestly unfair. He had probably thought he was merely following normal practice.'

And then again, one had to be realistic. To proceed in too draconian a fashion might have left the Police Force so denuded of staff as to constitute a threat to public order.

It was not the way to achieve things. The Egyptian tradition had always been to combine the threat of severity with the practice of clemency. The possibility of severity was always real and if, occasionally, by chance, that was what they got in the end and not clemency, well, that was the working of fate and seen not as injustice but as God deciding to exact full measure this time. You could hardly complain about that! If, on the other hand, the threat of severity was always followed by the practice of severity, people would perceive that as most unjust. It did not give fate a chance to work on your side, it allowed no escape for human compassion or indulgence. The system would be perceived as cold and inhuman. Not everyone understood that, said Philipides pointedly.

Mahmoud, whose logic tended towards the severely linear, was probably one of those. However, Philipides's remark was not directed at him.

'They come in from overseas,' he said bitterly, 'and they think we don't know how to do things, when it's just that we're doing them in a different way.'

'You are talking of Garvin effendi?'

Philipides hesitated but then committed himself.

'If he had been more patient,' he said, 'he would have seen that it was not as he supposed.'

'You are saying you are innocent of the charges?'

'Garvin effendi refused to believe that we were merely setting a trap. And I ask myself why he refused to believe us.'

'And what answer do you give?'

Philipides lifted his head and looked Mahmoud in the eyes.

'Because we were Egyptian,' he said; 'because we stood in the British way; because he wanted our places.'

Mahmoud said nothing but gave him the transcript to read.

The mouth beneath the moustache twitched painfully.

'How does this square with your story?'

'It does not contradict it,' said Philipides defiantly.

'No? "He can tell them things that lead to us"?'

'I was afraid that it would look as if we really were accepting money in exchange for promotion.'

'But why should you be concerned about that? Surely, all you had to do was go to Garvin effendi and tell him this was an official inquiry?'

'I was afraid he would not believe me.'

'You could have referred him to your superior.'

'I was working on this occasion for the Mamur Zapt.'

'Why was that?'

'It was an inquiry into the police. Wainwright Pasha wanted it to be someone independent. He did not know how far it might involve senior officers. There were rumours –'

'Rumours?'

'About Garvin effendi. Some jewels. A present for his wife.'

Mahmoud glanced at Owen, then made a note.

'But you, too,' he said to Philipides, 'were a member of the police, and if not a senior one, an important middle-ranking one.'

'Mustapha Mir thought he needed help.'

'Had he not men of his own?'

'No. Well, yes, but they were special men. He needed someone inside the Police Force.'

'Why did he choose you?'

'I had worked with him before. He trusted me.'

'Was this authorized by Wainwright Pasha?'

'Oh yes.'

'And known by Garvin effendi?'

'He knew I had worked with Mustapha Mir before, yes, but he did not know about this operation. That is why I was worried, why I telephoned Mustapha Mir –'

'I do not understand this,' said Mahmoud. 'If it was as you say, why was not the matter quickly cleared up? Surely, all Mustapha Mir had to do was get in touch with Garvin?'

'He knew he wouldn't believe him. That is why he went to Wainwright Pasha.'

Philipides glanced at the transcript.

'Look!' he said, pointing with his finger. 'It says there that he is going to see Wainwright Pasha.'

'In that case, why did not Wainwright Pasha speak to Garvin?'

'He did. But Garvin effendi did not believe him.'

'Did not believe him?' said Mahmoud incredulously. 'But surely Garvin effendi was Wainwright Pasha's deputy at the time?'

'He was. There was a terrible argument. And then Garvin effendi went over Wainwright Pasha's head.'

'To the Ministry of Justice?' said Mahmoud, puzzled. 'But that is not in my files.'

He looked at the big pile of folders on his desk.

'Not to the Ministry of Justice,' said Philipides. 'To the British Consul-General.'

'Ah! Oh, I see.'

'Wainwright Pasha spoke up strongly for Mustapha Mir. He said it was an injustice. But it was no good. They wanted Mustapha out, you see. That was what it was all about. He saw it at once. That was why he kept asking me if there were others or if it was just Garvin effendi alone. I did not understand, I was just a lowly inspector, I do not know about these things. But Mustapha Mir was clever, he did know about such things and he saw at once what was happening –'

'Just one moment,' said Mahmoud. 'What is it exactly that you are saying?'

'That there was a plot,' said Philipides determinedly, 'a British plot. That Garvin effendi saw an opportunity to discredit Mustapha Mir and force him out.'

'Why would he do that?'

'So that,' said Philipides bitterly, looking at Owen, 'his place could be taken by an Englishman.'

'A lot of nonsense,' said Owen, when they were alone.

'Is it?' said Mahmoud.

'Yes,' said Owen, 'it certainly is.'

'I'm not so sure,' said Mahmoud. 'Garvin is an ambitious man.'

'It wouldn't have been Mustapha Mir's job that he wanted,' Owen pointed out. 'It would have been Wainwright's.'

'And he got it,' said Mahmoud.

'That was later. That was nothing to do with this.'

Mahmoud, however, looked thoughtful.

'There are obvious weaknesses in the story,' said Owen.

Mahmoud nodded.

'Yes, but I will have to check them. I will have to investigate his accusations too, though.' He looked at Owen. 'That means going through the files.'

'Whose files?'

'Yours, perhaps,' said Mahmoud. 'Or rather, Mustapha Mir's.'

Owen was silent. There was a lot of secret material in the Mamur Zapt's files. Would the Administration agree?

'More to the point,' said Mahmoud, 'I shall have to go through the Commandant's files. Did Wainwright authorize Mustapha Mir to conduct an investigation into corruption in the Police Force? If he did, there ought to be some reference to it in the files.'

'Garvin's sitting on those files now,' said Owen.

'I shall have to ask him to release them.'

Owen was silent again. Garvin, he felt sure, had nothing to hide, but he might well object to opening his files to the Parquet. It was the principle of the thing, he would say. The Commandant of the Cairo Police was such an important post that its incumbent was appointed directly by the Khedive, not by the Minister of Justice. There was a reason for that. The Ministry was responsible for the administration of justice; but the Commandant was responsible for maintaining order, and the Khedive cared a lot more about maintaining order than he did about justice.

It could be put, too, another way. The Khedive appointed the Commandant on the direct advice of the British Administration, and the British were even more interested in maintaining order than they were in the administration of justice. The niceties of the legal administration they were quite happy to leave to the Egyptians; the exercise of power, though, they wished to keep to themselves.

The British Administration was advisory only. In theory, the Khedive and his ministers could reject that advice. In practice, because of the Egyptian Government's financial dependence on Britain, and because of the large British army stationed in Egypt, the advice was not something the Egyptians could easily disregard.

The British were punctilious in observing the advisory form. On the one hand it gave them something they could shelter behind; on the other, it saved the Khedive's self-respect.

Up to a point. As the years went by, and memory of the financial crisis receded into the background, the Khedive became increasingly restless. So did ambitious ministers. And so, much, much more so, did the growing forces of Egyptian Nationalism. There were many now, especially among the young professionals, who were eager to challenge the advisory form, to bring matters to a head over whether the British were here as advisers only or whether they were here to rule by force. The young lawyers of the Parquet, for instance. Mahmoud.

Like Garvin, Mahmoud might well see this as an issue of principle. Was the Commandant of the Cairo Police Force subject to the same judicial process as everyone else in Egypt or not? Did he answer to the Khedive and the National Assembly and the Ministry of Justice? Or only to the British?

'It may be necessary to interview Wainwright Pasha,' said Mahmoud.

'Wainwright? He left the country years ago!'

'He is still alive? These are grave charges,' said Mahmoud. 'He will have to come back.'

'Come back?' said Paul incredulously. 'Wainwright? Fat chance of that! He'll be too busy watering his roses, or whatever you do to roses.'

'If we cover his expenses.'

'Mahmoud's very free with my money,' said Paul.

'He might jump at it. A holiday in Egypt at the Government's expense.'

'Wainwright may be daft,' said Paul. 'But he's not as daft as that!'

'Mahmoud seems very determined,' said Owen. 'I think the Ministry might make a formal request.'

'Well, it will get a formal answer,' said Paul. 'Plus an informal one: Ha! Ha!'

'It's an issue of principle.'

'Is it hell!' said Paul. 'It's a matter of practice. How do you compel a chap to come back if he doesn't want to? Appeal to his better nature? Anyone who's served in the British Administration hasn't got one. Compel him legally? That would mean working through the Egyptian legal system, which is some task, I can tell you, especially when you get lawyers on to the job. And then it would have to go through the British legal system, which is even worse. It would take years. Wainwright would have died by the time it got to court. Of course, you could always bribe him, but that, given the nature of the investigation, hardly seems the appropriate thing to do. It might be worth trying, though. Since he's on a Government pension, he's bound to be short of money.'

'I'll put the suggestion to Mahmoud.'

'Actually,' said Paul, thinking, 'there's another issue of principle involved, too. It is; once you've retired, ought they to be able to get you for the things you've done?

Assert that as a principle and the prisons will be full of old age pensioners. No administrator will ever take a decision on anything. It's only because they think they'll be retired by the time there's any comeback that they take the decisions they do. No,' said Paul, shaking his head, 'this will not do. Mahmoud is tampering with sacred things. The principle of wiping the slate clean when you retire is fundamental to our society. Abolish it and the Western way of life falls apart.'

'You think there's no chance then?'

'It's Mahmoud *v* the Rest of the World. Again, poor chap.'

'Access to my files?' said Garvin. 'He'll be lucky!'

'Not so much yours as Wainwright's.'

Garvin shook his head.

'Impossible. Can't separate them. Besides, isn't there a question of principle?'

'Access to the files?' said Nikos, shocked, standing in front of the cabinets as if an immediate attack was about to be made on their honour. 'Never!'

'Only those dating back to Mustapha Mir's time,' said Owen.

'All destroyed,' said Nikos. 'It's an important principle. When you leave office you destroy all your papers. Anyone with any intelligence knows that.'

'Did Wainwright know that?'

'Well, of course, Wainwright —'

'There may not have been any papers,' Owen said to Mahmoud. 'And if there were, there won't be now.'

He found Zeinab fastening a necklace around her neck. It was a silver chain with pendant razzmatazz dangling from the front of it which sparkled and flashed in the lamplight.

'Very nice!' he said, kissing her just above the pendant.

Zeinab examined herself in the mirror.

'Yes,' she said, 'it suits me quite well. You don't usually have such good taste, darling.'

'What?' said Owen.

Zeinab put her arms round his neck and kissed him.

'Thank you, darling,' she said. 'We haven't seen each other for at least two days and I was just beginning to think that in your absent-minded way you had completely forgotten about me, when you produce something like this!'

'Just a minute!' said Owen.

Zeinab released him.

'Something wrong?'

'It doesn't come from me.'

'Oh!'

She sat down on the divan. After a moment she reached up and unfastened the necklace.

'Another admirer?'

'Shut up!' said Zeinab, and threw the necklace on the floor.

He tried to make amends by kissing her but she turned her head away.

'Perhaps your father sent it,' he suggested.

'When he gives me presents he likes to give me them directly.'

'Or one of his friends?'

It always worried Owen that one day Nuri Pasha might seek to marry his daughter off. Nuri was a westernized Francophile but you never knew in a thing like this and there had been recent signs that he was prepared to use his daughter to cement a political alliance.

'Marbrouk, for instance?'

'Don't be ridiculous! He's still on the Riviera. Where he went at your suggestion.'

'What about that new man your father seemed very thick with the other night at the Khedive's reception?'

'Demerdash Pasha?'

'That's right. The pro-Turk one.'

'He's not pro-Turk,' said Zeinab, 'he's pro-Khedive. Khedive as he was twenty years ago.'

'That's the one.'

'Just because my father flirts with him,' said Zeinab coldly, 'that doesn't mean he flirts with me.'

'All right, all right. I just thought an alliance might be in the making.'

'If it was,' said Zeinab, 'I don't think Demerdash would think of consulting me. Or that it was necessary to placate me with gifts.'

Owen picked up the necklace. It felt heavy. That sometimes meant such things were genuine silver.

'Whoever sent it will find a way of letting you know, won't they?'

'Why? Would you kill them?'

'Not exactly, but —'

Zeinab was disappointed.

'You English,' she complained, 'lack passion.'

'Let me convince you otherwise,' said Owen.

The Aalima's house, or perhaps he should call it coven, was a small modest building in a respectable part of the Gamaliya. Inside, however, it was surprisingly well furnished, with carpets on the walls, several low, well-cushioned divans and an unusual profusion of knick-knacks: fine porcelain lamp bowls, copper and silver trays and little silver filigree boxes. A brazier with a coffee pot was already waiting. Witch, she might be, but she knew how to behave.

She was, this time, decently veiled. Only the fine eyes were visible to remind Owen of the striking face. The matronly bearing, however, remained. Owen was shepherded firmly to one of the divans and given a cup of coffee. The Aalima sat down opposite; alone. She plainly had no truck with the usual convention which required a male family friend to be present when conversation was had with a lady.

'Well?' she said.

Owen discarded the smooth introduction he had prepared.

'Did you know the Bimbashi was going to be there?' he asked.

'No,' said the Aalima firmly.

'Then how was it you had the drug ready?'

The Aalima started to speak then stopped, as if changing her mind.

'We always have drugs,' she said. 'They are part of the ceremony. We use different ones at different times. This was one we normally use late on: if someone is over-excited.'

'Why, then, was it given to the Bimbashi?'

The Aalima's eyes flashed.

'It was none of his business!' she said angrily. 'It was not right that he should be there. I could not have done everything if he had been watching, I would not have been able to complete the ceremony.'

'So you sent him to sleep?'

'What is wrong with that?'

'You gave him too much. You could have killed him.'

The Aalima hesitated.

'We had no wish to kill him. If we gave him too much it was because we wished to make sure. We were not used to giving such doses.'

Owen nodded.

'The girl,' he said, 'Jalila; she put it in?'

'Jalila? No. She merely carries the bowl.'

'Did you put it in yourself?'

'It was part of the ceremony,' she said evasively.

'No matter; you are the one who will be held responsible.'

'He should not have come,' she said.

'I know; and therefore I am prepared to be lenient with you. Give me the information I want and you need hear no more of this.'

'What information do you want?'

'Let me ask my first question again. Did you know the Bimbashi would be there?'

'No,' she said. 'I knew only that he might be.'

'Who gave you that information?'

'I cannot say. Truthfully,' she added quickly. 'These things come to one, some words muttered in the *suk*, and one does not always see who has spoken. One only knows afterwards that they are important by the gift.'

'There was a gift?'

The Aalima inclined her head.

'What were the words?'

'A man might come.'

'There must have been more words than that.'

'No. Only that a man would come, a foolish Effendi, and I would know him when I saw him.'

'What were you to do?'

The Aalima hesitated.

'I was to let him stay,' she said reluctantly. 'I was to let him see.'

'No more?' said Owen, puzzled.

'Isn't that enough?'

'There was nothing else?'

'Nothing, I swear.'

'You have sworn,' said Owen, 'and I accept your word. If it turns out that you have forsworn, I must warn you that it will go heavy with you.'

'I have not forsworn. That was all that was said. And,' said the Aalima, 'I did not do what I was bid.'

'You did not let him see?'

'Not all. Some, yes, but not all. I could not bring myself to do it. The present they gave me was good, yes, but all the gold in the world – '

'I understand.'

'When I saw him there, and saw that he was looking, after he had said that he would not, I was angry and told – '

'Them to put in the drug?' Owen finished.

'Yes,' said the Aalima, looking at him defiantly.

Owen took his time about replying. He sipped his coffee carefully and then put the cup down on the little copper tray beside him.

'That, I could understand,' he said softly, 'although it was wrong; but why put him in the snake pit?'

'That was nothing to do with me.'

'Did you not give instructions?'

'No.'

'Who did?'

'I do not know.'

'Come,' said Owen, 'the Bimbashi was in the inner courtyard, where there were only those who follow you. Would they have done this without your command?'

'It was done,' said the Aalima, 'and I did not know it was done. I looked and saw that he was asleep and that was enough. I had my duties to think of.'

'Who commands in the courtyard?'

'No one commands,' said the Aalima. 'We are women and at the Zzarr we are free people. Only at the Zzarr.'

'I cannot believe that it was done without your knowledge.'

The Aalima shrugged.

'I have told you truly,' she said.

'Very well. Again I shall believe you. But tell me now,' said Owen, 'if you do not know, who would?'

The Aalima seemed genuinely to be thinking.

'Jalila?'

The Aalima gestured impatiently. 'She merely carries the bowl.'

'She was out in the courtyard.'

'True, but . . . it would have had to have been someone else. She does not command enough respect.'

'She may have seen.'

'Others must have seen,' said the Aalima. 'The chair was in the courtyard. But –'

'Yes?'

'They may have seen,' said the Aalima, 'but I do not think they would have done it. He is a heavy man for women to carry. Especially that far into the Gamaliya. And who would have been willing to leave the ceremony?'

'Men?' suggested Owen.

'There were no men in the courtyard,' said the Aalima definitely, 'apart from the Bimbashi. I will tell you what I will do,' she said. 'I will ask my women. And then I will tell you.'

'Thank you,' said Owen, rising. 'That is all I ask.'

As she was showing him out, he said to her: 'Why the snake pit? Are snakes something to do with the Zzarr?'

'The only snakes at the Zzarr,' said the Aalima, 'are men.'

8

It was only half past ten and the city was already like an oven. Inside the offices it was even worse and Owen, eager as always to keep things in perspective, headed for the café. Just as he was about to sit down, he saw Mahmoud and waved to him to join him. Mahmoud, however, did not notice and went hurrying on past. Owen waved again and then went across to intercept him. Reluctantly, Mahmoud came to a stop.

His face had none of its usual alertness and vigour. It was pinched and withdrawn.

'Hello!' said Owen, recognizing the signs. 'What's up?'

'Nothing,' said Mahmoud. 'Nothing.'

He tried to smile and failed, then began to edge away.

'Got something on,' he muttered.

'No you haven't,' said Owen, putting his arm around him. Arabs were always putting their arms round each other. If you didn't, you struck them as cold and unfriendly.

'Coffee,' said Owen. 'Come on!'

He shepherded Mahmoud back to his table. Mahmoud allowed himself to be persuaded but looked at Owen without any light in his eyes. Indeed, he seemed almost hostile.

'What's the trouble?' said Owen.

'Nothing,' said Mahmoud coldly.

'I know you too well to believe that,' said Owen.

The waiter, unusually, came quickly with the coffee. Mahmoud took a sip which was almost like a spit.

'Do you?' he said. 'Do you?'

Owen laid his hand on Mahmoud's arm.

'Come on,' he said, 'what's the matter?'

Mahmoud sat huddled and silent. When he was like this he was peculiarly exasperating. Normally he was so full of bounce that a chair could hardly contain him. On occasion, though, he swung to the other extreme, crumpling into apathy and lifelessness. You might have thought he suffered from some polarizing or cyclical illness; but the Arabs were all like this. They either burned with exhilaration or collapsed into the dumps; not like the stable British, who remained puddingy throughout.

They had been talking in French. Now Owen switched to the more intimate Arabic.

'If my brother is troubled,' he said, 'then I am troubled. And if he does not tell me his trouble, so that I can share it, then I am doubly troubled.'

Mahmoud said nothing for some time. When he replied, however, it was in Arabic, which was a kind of response.

'You cannot share,' he said, 'because you cannot feel.'

'That is unjust,' said Owen quietly.

Mahmoud shifted uncomfortably.

'It is not your fault,' he said. 'It is because you are an Englishman.'

Oh no, thought Owen, so that's what it is.

'Have you forgotten so soon?' he said reproachfully. 'I am not an Englishman.'

Something stirred down in the dumps. Arab, Mahmoud might be, and liable to plunge into the trough of depression; but Arab, he still was, and unable to forgive himself for anything that seemed a breach of courtesy. He raised a hand apologetically.

'I am not always clear,' he said, 'about the difference between an Englishman and a Welshman.'

'This is fighting talk,' said Owen.

Mahmoud managed something that was a little like a smile. He took a sip of coffee, looked at it with surprise and took another sip.

'What have we done this time?' asked Owen.

'We? I thought you were a Welshman?' said Mahmoud, beginning to sparkle.

'We have a pact with them.'

'If you have, it's a pact with the devil.'

'Are things that bad?'

'Well –'

Mahmoud looked round and waved for more coffee. He was beginning to brisk up. That was a good sign. Mahmoud, in normal form, had all the briskness and sharpness of a mongoose.

'They won't give me access,' he said.

'Access?'

'To the files. It is quite improper. To refuse a request from the Ministry of Justice, from the Government. Whose country do they think this is?'

'Hold on. Whose files are we talking about?'

'Garvin's, Wainwright's, Mustapha Mir's. Yours.'

'I haven't refused you access.'

'Haven't you?'

'I'm still thinking about it.'

'It's not going to be up to you. An in-principle decision has been taken. By the Consul-General.'

'I'll have a word with Paul.'

'It'll be no good. This goes deep, you see. It raises big questions. The biggest,' said Mahmoud bitterly, 'is: who governs this country? And we know the answer to that, don't we?'

Owen tried to think what to say. Mahmoud, however, was not expecting a reply.

'It's the principle of the thing,' he said vehemently. 'It is fundamental to the administration of justice. The investigating officer must have access to relevant documents. No one, no one should be able to refuse. No one should be above the law. Neither I nor you, nor the Khedive, nor the British. We are all equal before the law. Everyone! That is what justice *is*.'

'Yes,' said Owen, 'but this is Egypt.'

'It doesn't matter. It should make no difference.'

'It is the difference,' said Owen, 'between an ideal and reality.'

'Yes, but,' said Mahmoud, all excited now, 'on this there must be no compromise. Or where shall we be? One law for one, one for another' – forgetting that in Egypt there were at least three legal systems – 'No!' He banged his fist on the table. The cups jumped. Owen looked around apprehensively; but other people, all over the place, seemed to be banging their fists too. It was the normal mode of Arab conversation. They were probably talking about something as innocuous as the weather. 'We cannot have it!' shouted Mahmoud. 'Not as Egyptians, no, nor as English, but as part of mankind! It is our right!'

He banged his fist so fiercely that even some of the other bangers looked round.

'And as Welshmen, too,' added Mahmoud, a little self-consciously.

What was he going to do? Owen asked himself. Not about Mahmoud's depression – he was bouncing out of it now and was once more rearing to go – but about the issue of principle? The Consul-General had defined it and that ought to have been the end of it for any member of the British Administration. But Owen wasn't, or, at least, not quite, entirely a member of the British Administration and interpreted himself as having some degree of latitude. He didn't have to go along with it if he didn't want to.

'Why don't they let me investigate?' cried Mahmoud, firing up again. 'Have they something to hide?'

'I doubt it. It's just the normal bureaucratic reaction.'

'Is it that they do not trust me?' demanded Mahmoud fiercely.

'No, no, no, no. It's nothing like that.'

Except that in a way it was. Every administrator – and Owen was one himself – developed a kind of plural sense of the truth. They knew the truth had more than one side. The difference between Owen and the others, however, was that whereas for them there were only two sides – their Department's and anyone else's – for him there were so many sides that he couldn't keep up with them. Mahmoud, on the other hand, believed that there was only one truth, which it was his job to discover.

People who felt like that were always difficult to deal with. They recognized everybody else's partiality but not their own. They made, however, very good investigators.

'They look down on me,' said Mahmoud, 'because I am an Egyptian!'

'Nonsense!'

He knew, however, that he would have to do something.

'I'll tell you what,' he said: 'you can look at my files.'

Mahmoud stopped in his rhetorical tracks.

'I can?'

'Or rather, Mustapha Mir's. Those relating to that period. The ones we can find,' he amended, remembering what Nikos had said.

'That will be something,' said Mahmoud. 'That, in fact, would be a great help.'

'I hope so.'

'But, look,' said Mahmoud, remembering that Owen was his friend, and concerned, 'I don't want to get you into trouble.'

'That's all right.'

'How will you get round the Consul-General's ruling?'

'No one's told me about it yet,' said Owen. 'By the time they do, it might be too late.'

'No one's said anything about it yet.'

The necklace hung casually on a hook beside Zeinab's dressing table. It had not been admitted to the silver box where she kept her bracelets, rings and other jewellery.

'That's funny,' said Owen, picking it up. 'You'd have expected someone to have claimed the credit by now.'

'Or the reward?'

'There isn't going to be a reward,' said Owen firmly.

'No?'

Zeinab put the necklace back on the hook; which was exactly where she liked to keep Owen.

'You're right, though,' he said, reflecting. 'No one gives something for nothing. The question is: what reward did they have in mind?'

'I'd have thought that was obvious,' said Zeinab.

'That's what I thought, too. But the fact that they haven't come forward is making me think again.'

'What else could it be?'

'Either it's part of some deal your father is cooking up –'

'Forget about my father. He usually tells me if he's thinking of me marrying someone.'

'– or else, or else, it's not really to do with you at all, it's –'

'Yes?'

'It's something to do with me.'

'Oh, come, darling –'

'It's like those earrings. The ones that were sent to Garvin. Or rather, to Garvin's wife.'

He told her about them. Zeinab listened seriously.

'First the diamond,' she said, 'then this. I think you ought to go a bit carefully, darling. For a while.'

'Yes, you're right. We ought to be a bit careful with the necklace. See it's kept somewhere.'

'Your pocket, perhaps?' suggested Zeinab.

The Aalima, straight-backed and veiled, was waiting to receive him. The coffee pot was already standing on the low table beside the divan and the pleasant aroma of the coffee filled the room. The shutters were closed because of the intense heat, but enough light came through the slots to make it unnecessary to use a lamp.

The Aalima was more relaxed this time and conversation was conducted at a proper pace. Owen fell naturally into the long, graceful Arabic salutations and then gradually, feigning proper reluctance, allowed himself to be persuaded to sip his coffee, praising it copiously. One of the things he liked about visiting Egyptians was that their courteous insistence on observing the forms reduced everything to a slow rhythm. Owen was all in favour of slow rhythms, especially in heat like this.

They discussed the hot spell and wondered when it would end; and little by little the conversation turned to the point of his visit.

'I have done what you wished,' said the Aalima at last. 'I have asked my women what happened in the courtyard that night.'

'And?'

The Aalima frowned.

'It is bad,' she said. 'I wish I had never agreed. Either to their suggestion that I let him see or to his own insistence. It was bad. And bad comes to bad.'

'It was bad to drug him, certainly.'

'What followed was worse. Men came into the courtyard.'

'Is not that forbidden?'

'They said they had my word. My women knew that I had made some agreement and thought that this was part of it. That is what I meant when I said that bad leads to bad.'

'They used you for their own ends.'

'That is always the way,' said the Aalima, 'with men.'

Owen said nothing.

'It spoiled it,' said the Aalima. 'It destroyed the sanctity of the Zzarr. I should not have agreed. Now I shall have to do it again.'

'You have, of course, done it again, and I hope my presence did not spoil it that time.'

'We shall have to see. All I know is that what I did the first time was not successful.'

'The spirits remained after?'

The Aalima inclined her head.

'Not surprisingly,' she said.

'What did your women see?'

'Men came into the courtyard. They took the Bimbashi on his chair and carried him out.'

116

'Did they know the men?'

The Aalima shook her head.

'Would they know them again?'

'It was dark.'

'They carried him out of the courtyard. Did your women see where they carried him to?'

The Aalima hesitated.

'This is the worst part,' she said. 'They carried him back into the outer courtyard.' She looked at Owen. 'So that everyone could see.'

'I do not understand.'

'They showed him to those who were there. They raised him on his chair.'

Still Owen did not understand.

'There were people in the courtyard?'

'Many.'

'And McPhee was . . . displayed?'

'Yes. They said: "See how the Zzarr has been violated! And see who has done it!"'

'No one has told me this.'

'I did not know it either,' said the Aalima, 'until I asked.'

Sheikh Musa sighed.

'Well, of course!' he said. 'That was exactly the problem. After that there could be no denying it. Everyone had seen. I did my best. I tried to play it down. "Zzarr?" I said. "What Zzarr? The church does not know any such thing." Which was all very well, except that everyone else did. To deny that there had been a Bimbashi as well would have been too much. It would have been like performing a sort of inverse miracle.'

Owen found himself warming to the Sheikh.

'I very much regret any difficulty or embarrassment this has caused you,' he said.

The Sheikh shrugged and spread his hands.

'I don't suppose he intended it,' he said.

'The very last thing he would have wished would have been to cause offence.'

'Maybe,' said the Sheikh; 'but he was there, wasn't he?'

'He was brought there by a trick.'

'Why would anyone wish to do that?' asked Sheikh Musa. 'I could understand if it had been a mosque. There are always those who wish to fan the flames of religious division. But a Zzarr? Why a Zzarr?'

'Because they knew McPhee would come to it. If it had been a mosque or anything to do with orthodox religious practice he wouldn't have touched it. He has great, genuine respect for such matters and knows too much about them to be inveigled into doing something that would offend. But a Zzarr, well, a Zzarr would be different. For him it is the past, from the days before there was Islam or even Christianity. That kind of thing fascinates him.'

'If they knew that about him,' said Sheikh Musa, 'then they must have known him well.'

He had gone to the Sheikh hoping that he could have put him into touch with people who had been present in the outer courtyard that night and who had seen the whole thing. After considerable hesitation — the Sheikh, like Owen, still had hopes that the whole thing would die away and be quietly forgotten, and had no wish to do anything which might resurrect sleeping embers — he had reluctantly agreed to let Owen meet two suitable members of his flock. They had certainly been present; unfortunately, they had been chosen for their trustworthiness and discretion rather than for their ability to convey their impressions of what they had seen, and he got little out of them.

Yes, the Bimbashi had been brought out into the outer courtyard and lifted up on a chair so that he could be clearly seen by all who were present. 'In the torchlight,' one of them added. 'Drunk,' said the other.

'Not drunk,' said Owen, 'drugged.'

The two remained unconvinced.

'In a thing like this,' said the Sheikh afterwards, 'people believe what is said at the time.'

Owen asked about the men. They came from outside the Gamaliya. The two were quite sure of this. Most Cairenes, probably wisely, were sure of this sort of fact whenever it fell to their lot to witness a crime. Owen did not insist.

But what had happened to McPhee at the end, after he had been shown to the assembled population? He had been taken away, the men said vaguely. Who by? The same men? Probably. Couldn't they remember anything about it? Nothing at all. How many men had there been, Owen asked desperately? Four. Or rather two. Plus one who had led them. Three, then? The men conferred. You might say that; yes, you might say that. What was this other one like? A lowly man, they said with scorn. Lowly? Definitely. A fellah? Worse than that. But was not that strange, a mere fellah, and a leader? Ah, well, he hadn't exactly been their leader, at least, not like that, more one who had shown them the way. He had known the way, then, himself? Seemed to. And the others had not? Definitely not. They were from outside the Gamaliya. And the other one? The one who had led? Couldn't see, it was dark, etc., etc.

So he *had* come from the Gamaliya. In fact, he must have known the Gamaliya well to have been able to guide the men into a backyard and then to the cistern into which they had dropped McPhee.

That wasn't the sort of place you hit on by accident as you were fleeing. McPhee must have been dropped there deliberately, as a kind of cruel joke. Which suggested that the man, the lowly one who had guided them, had known it was there.

Owen decided to go and see Jalila.

The yard was busy now. Semi-finished screens for the large, box-like windows which were a feature of old Cairo were propped up everywhere with men bent over them applying the final touches. Elsewhere, men were working on earlier stages. In one corner they were doing the preliminary sawing, holding the wood in their toes; in another they were turning the pegs with little pigmy-like bows. All the work was being done on the ground, none on benches.

Owen greeted the men politely and asked for Jalila. You did not usually ask for women by name – in fact, you did not usually ask for women at all – but snake-catchers' daughters were different. One of the men went to the back of the yard and called up to a window at the top of some wooden stairs. A moment later, Jalila appeared.

'There's an Effendi here who wishes to speak with you, Jalila.'

'Oh, it's you,' said Jalila, pleased, and came down the stairs.

'Posh friends our Jalila's got!' one of the workmen said to another.

'He's probably been showing her a snake. Or something,' said the other.

As Jalila went past the cistern she put her arm down into it and scooped out a snake; which she promptly threw in the direction of the speakers.

There was pandemonium in the yard as the workmen dropped their work and jumped hastily out of the way. Jalila stood for a moment, hands on hips, enjoying the panic, then walked across, picked up the snake and put it back in the cistern.

'I hope that one was milked,' said Owen.

'Maybe,' said Jalila. 'Maybe not.'

'Can we talk?'

Jalila led him up the stairs and then up another flight round the side of the building and so on to the roof. Some rolled up mattresses suggested that like many Cairo roofs, especially in hot weather, it was used for sleeping.

'You were not, of course, up here the night the Bimbashi was put in the cistern?'

'I was at the Zzarr.'

'Of course. Was – was –' he was not sure of her circumstances – 'anyone else up here?'

'My father was sleeping with Ali Haja's widow. In another house.'

'I was wondering if anyone had heard anything. People on other roofs, perhaps.'

'If they did, no one has said so.'

'Isn't that strange? A hot night, in the open. Surely someone must have heard.'

'No one has said anything. I do not know if that is strange.'

'It is, of course, possible that no one heard anything. If that were so it would be because the men came quietly. And if that were so, it would be because they knew their way, or at least, one of them did.'

'Many people know the yard.'

'And the cistern?'

'They might if they had come here on business. To see my father.'

Owen was disappointed. He had hoped he was narrowing things down.

'Even so,' he said, 'it means they must have known the Gamaliya. More, this part of the Gamaliya. And I think that is true, for they knew of the Aalima, and they knew which house was the Copt's.'

Jalila wriggled her toes. Not surprisingly, thought Owen. The roof was so hot that even to put your hand on it was painful.

Jalila was bare-faced as well as bare-footed. Interesting, that. Poor women usually wore a veil. Perhaps snake-catchers' daughters were so low in the social hierarchy that they fell even below that level.

Jalila, now he came to consider it, had a pleasant face, not Arab-aquiline like Zeinab's but broad and round.

'Where does your father come from, Jalila?' he asked.

'Here.'

'And his father?'

'Here. We have always been here.'

'It is the face. It does not seem a northern face.'

'They say we originally came from Suakin.'

121

'Ah!'

A port city. Therefore, probably mixed. He fancied he saw something Somali in her features.

'You like my face?'

'Yes. It is a pretty one.'

Jalila wriggled her toes again.

'I like this kind of conversation,' she said.

'Don't get much of it among the snakes, I suppose.'

A woman came out on to a roof opposite.

'That's your reputation gone!'

'My father will beat me, perhaps.'

'Tell him the Mamur Zapt says that would be unwise.'

'If I tell him that, he will be troubled. He thinks it best to have nothing to do with the great.'

'A wise man. A wise daughter, too, and that is why I have come to you. Jalila, I need to know what happened in the courtyard the night the Bimbashi came.'

'He fell asleep.'

'You drugged him. That I know. It is the next bit that interests me. He was taken from the courtyard. How?'

'Men came.'

'Into the yard?'

'Yes. It is forbidden but they came all the same. The Aalima was very angry.'

'Did you see them?'

'Not well. I was on the other side of the courtyard. I had just filled my bowl. I heard the women cry out and I looked up and they were just lifting him, high up on their shoulders. And then they ran through the arch into the other courtyard.'

'What happened then?'

'I heard a great shout, and then men were crying out.'

'You did not see?'

She shook her head.

'The Aalima came out at that point. She called us to her and said: "What is this?" And we told her, and she was very angry.'

'How many men were there?'

'Five. Two of them were holding the chair. One was telling them what to do. The others – I do not know. Perhaps they were holding the chair, too.'

'The one who was telling them what to do: was he a lowly man?'

Jalila looked surprised.

'Lowly? Not especially.'

Oh, well. It might not have helped much – there were a lot of lowly men in Cairo – but it would have been nice to have had corroboration.

'Could you describe him to me?'

Not very well. It had been dark, she had seen them briefly and through a crowd. They had looked, well, ordinary. Big, perhaps. Would she recognize them if she saw them again? She shook her head doubtfully.

'Jalila, if you do see them – and you may see them, for one at least is from the Gamaliya – and you let me know, it will be to your advantage.'

'If I see them, I will let you know,' said Jalila, 'but it will not be for money.'

Mahmoud came to Owen's office that afternoon. It was the afternoon because it was then that the Bab-el-Khalk was empty and there would not be many to witness what Nikos considered his disgrace. He had, of course, demurred but Owen had not given him sufficient time to be able to organize his defences in terms either of a last-ditch appeal to higher authority or of tampering with the files. All he could do was sit and simmer.

When Mahmoud was shown in, he was distantly polite. There would be no confrontation – that was not Nikos's way – but there would be no assistance either. If Mahmoud could find what he wanted, well and good, or, rather, ill and bad, but he would have to find it for himself.

Mahmoud understood the situation perfectly and was courtesy itself. He also understood filing systems, which was something Nikos had not banked on and was particularly exasperating. A few minimal inquiries and he was on his way. Nikos folded his arms and settled down to watch. There was always the chance that Mahmoud would find it off-putting.

Provokingly, Mahmoud seemed entirely at ease.

Owen, prudently, left them to it and went away to work in his own office. Some three hours later, Mahmoud appeared in his doorway. A brooding Nikos hovered just behind him.

Mahmoud came in and put a piece of paper on his desk. It was an official memorandum and came from the Commandant of the Cairo Police. It said:

This is to confirm our conversation in my office this morning, namely that you are hereby authorized and instructed to conduct an inquiry into the degree and prevalence of corruption in the Cairo City Police Force.

It was addressed to Mustapha Mir, the Mamur Zapt, and was signed P. Wainwright, Commandant of Police.

9

Garvin dismissed it contemptuously.

'A cover-up,' he said. 'Wainwright was as weak as water. Mustapha Mir could twist him round his little finger. He wrote the memo himself and got Wainwright to sign it.'

'That may be,' Mahmoud said to Owen later, 'but you can't just dismiss it. On the face of it, it confirms Philipides's story: there *was* an investigation going on into the corruption in the Police Force, it *was* being conducted, quite properly, by the Mamur Zapt, and Philipides might well have been acting as *agent provocateur*. What evidence there is supports Philipides.'

'The two were in it together,' said Owen. 'Mustapha Mir and Philipides.'

'Three,' said Mahmoud. 'And Wainwright.'

'Mir could twist him round his little finger.'

'So Garvin keeps saying. But if he could,' said Mahmoud, 'it's the first case I've met of a senior British officer doing what an Egyptian told him.'

'You're not saying that Garvin is making this up?'

'I'm just following normal procedure,' said Mahmoud, 'checking the evidence. I've checked Philipides's and I've found it corroborated. I'll try and do the same for Garvin's. It doesn't help that he refuses me access to Wainwright's files.'

'All you'd find is a copy of the same memo.'

'I might find more. I might find evidence supporting the case that there was corruption in the Police Force.

Independent evidence. Independent, that is, of Mustapha Mir. I might find more detailed instructions frcm Wainwright. I might find a sketch by Mustapha Mir of how he intended to set about the investigation. It might even include the suggestion of using Philipides as an *agent provocateur.*'

'That wouldn't help Garvin.'

'I'm not trying to help Garvin. I'm trying to establish the truth. And when I find someone obstructing me from finding out the truth, I ask myself why. One answer is that they do not want me to find out the truth.'

'There are other answers. Issues of security, for instance.'

'I am an employee of the Ministry of Justice. Ultimately of the Khedive. As Garvin is. Cannot I be trusted on an issue of security? After all,' said Mahmoud, 'it is my country, not Garvin's.'

'He's taken it higher,' said Paul that evening in the bar. 'His Minister has formally asked the Khedive to instruct Garvin to release the files.'

'Much good that will do him,' said Owen.

'It's not as simple as that. It's put the Khedive on the spot. He knows Garvin won't release the files unless the Consul-General tells him. But if he asks the C-G and the C-G says no, that will be a smack in the face and won't do him any good with the Nationalists. He is in a considerable dither.'

'His normal state.'

'Forgivable, I think, this time. The C-G is not particularly happy about it, either, however. He doesn't want to have to say no because he doesn't want to be seen giving the Khedive a smack in the face. It doesn't look good to other countries. We're only supposed to be advisers. He's on the spot, too. The people back home think it's bad handling if issues like this are allowed to arise.'

'Everyone on the spot!' said Owen. 'Just because Mahmoud insists on doing his job.'

'It comes as a bit of a surprise, of course,' said Paul,

'when someone starts doing that. No one's ready for it. However, one result is that they start questioning how *other* people are doing their jobs. Me. You. You, after all, are supposed to be seeing that nothing awkward arises as a result of this investigation.'

'I'm not sure it was put quite like that,' protested Owen.

'We, at least, are not daft enough to write memos about it,' said Paul, 'but you know what I mean. Actually,' he said, waving for two more whiskies to sweeten the pill, 'there ought to be no question of either of you departing, provided matters are handled with dexterity.'

A little group of people came out on to the verandah, where Owen and Paul were sitting. Normally, it was cooler out there but tonight the temperature was like that of an oven. 'Cooler indoors,' said one of the group. 'Let's go back inside.' As he turned, one of the men saw Owen and Paul.

'Hello!' he said, dropping into a chair opposite them. 'What's this I hear about Wainwright? Coming back out here to give evidence or something?'

'Not so far as I know,' said Paul, 'not unless he's completely taken leave of his senses.'

'You remember Wainwright, of course?'

Paul shook his head.

'Before my time. Before yours, too, wasn't he?' he said to Owen.

'A couple of years before,' said Owen.

'Oh! Well, he was Chief of Police. Nice chap. Very active in the Horticultural Society. You should have seen his garden! Envy of all the rest of us, I can tell you. It will be nice to have him back. Pick his brain over my oleander.'

'I doubt, actually, if he'll come.'

'Oh? Pottinger seemed quite certain about it. His missus has had a letter from Wainwright's missus. She'll be coming too – the Khedive's paying, after all – and they've asked the Pottingers to put them up.'

'Kind of them,' said Paul.

'It'll be rather nice to have him around,' said his informant happily. 'We'll be able to talk over a thing or two.'

'It's a long way to come.'

'You'd think there was too much happening in the garden.'

'First thought that came into my head.'

'Decent chap, Wainwright. You never knew him?'

'Afraid not. A decent chap, you say?'

'Oh yes. He was our secretary for, well, it must have been nearly ten years. Everybody liked him. Always willing to do anyone a good turn.'

'I'm sure.'

'Nice chap. Straightforward.'

'Straightforward?' said Paul. 'Oh!'

The voice sounded familiar.

'Who are you?'

'A friend of Philipides.'

'Does Philipides wish to speak with me?'

'No. *I* wish to speak with you.'

'What about?'

'Philipides.'

He had placed the voice now. It was the girl who had been in his bed.

'Come to my office.'

'No.'

'Why not?'

'Philipides would hear.'

'Will he not hear if I come to your *appartement*?'

'It is not my *appartement*. It belongs to a friend.'

'If I come, you had better be sure I leave.'

'I know, I know,' said the voice impatiently. 'You will bring men. They will watch the house. You need not worry. There is only me.'

'Very well. I will come.'

'This evening, then.'

He decided to take Selim. Selim was not the brightest but he was the biggest. Selim, spotting another rung on the ladder, was ecstatic.

'Effendi,' he said, 'you can rely on me.'

'Give me an hour,' said Owen, 'and then break in.'

'Effendi, I will.'

Selim's confidence fell a little when he saw the building.

'Effendi,' he said, in worried tones, 'this is a bit high class. Are you sure I am to break in?'

'After an hour,' said Owen, 'you break in. There may be a chain on the door. Do you know how to handle that?'

'Oh yes, effendi. There was a chain on the door of a House for the Girls we called on last week and that was no problem.'

'An hour, then.'

The *appartement* was on an upper floor and there was a chain.

'Leave that,' said Owen, as she made to replace it after letting him in.

The girl shrugged. She was dressed in the mixed way of many Levantine girls, in a European dress but with a heavy black veil which concealed her hair and the lower part of her face. Owen could not help remembering her as she had been without either.

She led him into a dark inner room lavishly furnished with rich, thick carpets, on both floor and walls, and not much else apart from a low divan and an even lower table on which were coffee cups. Beside the table was a brazier with a coffee pot nestling in its top. Most of the light in the room came from the brazier but there was a small oil lamp in a niche in the wall.

The girl sat down at one end of the divan, nearest the brazier, and motioned to Owen to sit at the other. She poured him some coffee. Owen thanked her and put his lips to the cup but did not drink until he had seen her do so.

'My name is Mariam,' she said.

'You know my name.'

'Gareth.'

'My friends call me that.'

'Yes, Gareth.'

Owen was a little taken aback. Their relationship had, indeed, begun on an intimate note; but he was surprised to find that it had already progressed so far.

'You are also a friend of Philipides,' he said.

'I am his wife.'

'But –'

'Why are you surprised? Do you think it strange that a woman should wish to do what she could for her husband?'

'No, but I find it a little strange that she should wish to do what she could for someone else as well. Especially a casual stranger.'

'But you are not a casual stranger. Our lives are bound up.'

'I must admit that had escaped me up till now.'

'You are new to Cairo. All our lives are bound together.'

'Only up to a point.'

'More than you think. You have power over my husband. You have power over me.'

'I shall not exercise that power. Unless –'

'Ah, you see! It is that "unless".'

'What your husband did is past, paid for. I had nothing to do with it. I wasn't even here at the time. I only come into it if he does something new.'

'No,' she said. 'No. You have the power to alter the past. You can make things right.'

'Right?'

'They say you are a just man. A man of craft, yes, well, perhaps that is right, the Mamur Zapt has to be like that; Mustapha was –'

'You know Mustapha Mir?'

'Intimately. But that was in the past. But perhaps for him, too, it has to be put right.'

'What are you saying? That your husband was unjustly treated? That he was not guilty of the charges of corruption that were brought against him?'

'He was no more corrupt than anyone else.'

'That is not the point.'

'But it *is* the point. He was trying to change things from the inside. As Mustapha Mir was. It was a difficult position to be in. But he was honest. Corrupt, yes, but also honest. Wainwright Pasha had told Mustapha that things must be cleaned up, and that is what they were trying to do. But from the inside. It has to be from the inside if you wish to do anything in Egypt. You Effendis come and you sweep things away and put new things in their places, but the old things had their share of good and the new things do not work. Oh, you think they work, but they do not really. Your new ways only scratch the surface. If you want to get anywhere, you have to begin from within. That is what my husband was trying to do and you put him in prison –'

'The case is being reinvestigated.'

'I know. My husband said that you were there. But he said that you looked cold, that you did not understand. You see it through their eyes, the eyes of the Effendis, and not through our eyes, you do not see it as it was.'

'I will try to see it honestly.'

'No. That is not enough. You must see it sympathetically.'

'But that would be to prejudge –'

He stopped. Hadn't McPhee said something like this?

'I shall try to see with sympathy,' he concluded lamely.

'I hope so. They say you have the gift. But I do not know how that can be,' she said despondently. 'You are not part of Egypt.'

'You speak passionately for your husband.'

'I love him.'

'And yet you would have slept with me.'

'Because I love him.'

'That is not the way,' Owen reproved her; and he felt he sounded oddly like Garvin.

Selim was disappointed.

'I was just getting ready to come in,' he said.

'It wasn't necessary.'

131

Selim fell in step beside him.

'They say she's a beautiful woman,' he said enviously.

'Who?'

'Mustapha Mir's woman.'

'Not just Mustapha Mir's,' said Owen.

As they were walking back to the Bab-el-Khalk, Owen fancied he heard the sound of bagpipes. One of the Scottish regiments, he presumed; but, no, as he drew nearer he realized that it was the Egyptian sort. They turned a corner and saw a small crowd in front of them. The music was coming from the other side of the crowd. He could just see the pipes sticking up above the heads of the people before him. There was a sudden roll of a drum and a man began speaking.

'It is the Mohabazin,' said Selim delightedly.

They stopped to look. Cairo was a great place for street entertainment. There were dancers, jugglers, acrobats, snake charmers, of course, poets and singers. There were also the Mohabazin. These were small groups of actors who played in the streets and specialized in scurrilous farce. They were a kind of living Punch and Judy, often taking family life as their subject but also, not infrequently, offering a political commentary on the state of the nation and the ways of the great which was usually ribald and sometimes true.

There were, he could now see, two actors apart from the bagpipes player. One, whom he had not seen at first, was sitting on a chair. The actor, who was standing and doing most of the talking, was flourishing a big stick.

'Oh ho!' said Selim, 'it's the police this time, is it?'

The man with the stick strutted round and banged a few people with it. He was evidently a Selim sort of policeman. The crowd responded with repartee and jibes and some lively exchanges developed. Selim was splitting his sides some time before Owen got the hang of what they were saying. The 'policeman' was affecting to be a great hero; the crowd, egged on by the facial expressions of the man sitting on the chair, voiced doubts.

The policeman took their remarks as aspersions on his virility and responded indignantly, using the stick now to indicate his physical capacity. Female members of the audience were invited to put the matter to the test. They replied with derision, one lady producing a matchstick which was compared delightedly with the policeman's big stick. The policeman, hurt, announced that he was going home.

As he went, heroism and virility oozed away with every step until, after much hesitation, he brought himself to knock timidly on his front door, whereupon his wife came out in true Judy fashion and belaboured him thoroughly with his stick.

'Very good!' said Selim. 'Oh, very good!'

The man with the bagpipes made a collection while the actors prepared for the next piece by putting on different garb. It mostly concerned the man on the chair and did not amount to much: a tarboosh on his head, a red jacket with yellow pipes, which might have belonged to a bandsman, and a rag round his neck which conceivably represented a tie.

The bagpiper gave a skirl on his pipes and the next skit began. It had a different theme and centred this time on the man in the chair. He began turning round on his chair and pretending to peep at something over his shoulder. The peeps became longer and his eyes seemed about to pop out of his head. Affecting shock, horror – and delight – he covered his eyes with his hand and turned hastily away; only, a second or two later, for his head to swivel round once more and his eyes to pop again.

After the process had been repeated several times, the figure began to show signs of mounting sexual excitement. When he spun round now, he rose halfway up the chair and made exaggerated pelvic thrusts. He pantomimed heat, mopping his brow, loosening his tie and undoing his jacket.

It was not enough. He called for drink. The bagpipes player proffered him a bowl and he drank from it greedily. Evidently, it was alcoholic liquor, for he began, very funnily, to suggest growing intoxication. The crowd was in stitches as he swayed about, nearly falling off the chair, getting into a tangle with his tie and missing his buttons. Finally, highly excited by whatever it was that was behind him, he tried to take off his trousers – Selim liked this bit especially – tripped himself up over the legs, collapsed in a heap on the chair and promptly fell asleep.

The other actor and the bagpipes player seized the chair and held him aloft; and it was only then that Owen realized whom the figure on the chair was intended to represent: McPhee.

The next morning, Owen sat in his office thinking about it. Ordinarily, it wouldn't have bothered him. People were entitled to their bit of fun, after all, and the Cairo poor didn't get much of it. A little ridicule was healthy; not so nice, perhaps, when it was you that was being ridiculed but basically something that anyone in office ought to be tough enough to put up with. He was pretty sure that the Mamur Zapt figured in the Mohabazin's repertoire.

It meant, however, that his efforts to contain the episode through his control of the press had failed. Perhaps they were bound to. Owen had no illusions about the limits to his power in that respect. Things would always get out in the end. The most you could hope to do was to delay them.

That was what he had tried to do; that, and put a spoke in their wheel if there genuinely was somebody who was running a campaign against McPhee. Was that the case? Did the fact that the McPhee story was now being played on the streets mean there was somebody deliberately trying to put it about?

He wasn't sure. There was a gap between the culture of the written word, written though it might be in popular newspapers, and the life of the streets. Many people, perhaps most people, in Cairo could not read. The people who were inflamed by what they read in the newspapers were mostly students. It was they who came out on demonstrations. The ordinary Cairene-in-the-street went along to see the fun but unless religion came into it was not much involved.

Religion did come into it here, or could come into it if they weren't careful. But no one was going to get a fit of religion from watching one of the Mohabazin's plays. So even if someone was putting it about, was it worth bothering with? A little ridicule didn't hurt anyone and McPhee had bloody asked for it.

However, there was Garvin's point. There were, all told, only a handful of British in Egypt. The country was ruled, in effect, by a very tiny group of men. It was in a way a bluff; and it worked only as long as the bluff wasn't called. All right, there was an army offstage, but it was the fervent intention of every member of the Administration that that was exactly where it should stay. Bluff was the thing on which the Administration really depended; the kind of bluff that allowed three foreigners to run the Police Force and maintain order in a country the size of Egypt.

But one of the men was McPhee. And was McPhee the sort of man who could maintain the bluff convincingly? Not on present form. Garvin was right. Credibility was all.

Or was it? Hell, what did it matter if McPhee had become a bit of a joke? He was in danger of taking it all too seriously. It was this damned heat. You lost perspective. He decided he would go out for a coffee in an attempt to regain it.

He took the papers with him. As he went out, Nikos clapped another one on top of the pile.

'What's this?'

'*Al-Lewa.*'

'I've got it already.'

'You haven't got this one. This one is the one that actually came out this morning.'

'"Actually came out"? You mean it was not the one I approved?'

'Take a look,' said Nikos. 'I think you'll find it interesting.'

The article took up most of the front page. It was an attack on the Cairo Police Force. It began with general charges of inefficiency and incompetence (plenty of examples, including, yes, the one about the whole Police Force out one day recently looking for, wait for it, a *donkey*!) and then moved swiftly to the suggestion that this was the fault not of the ordinary constable (fine, upstanding, brave, true, diligent, conscientious to a fault, decent, highly moral – Selim?) but of his superiors, in particular those who had been imposed on the Police Force from overseas.

It was not just that they were corrupt, though there was abundant evidence of that, some of it going back a long time (earrings), some of it more recent (jewels given to whores), nor just that they were personally immoral; it was that they had been imposed by powers overseas for a purpose. That purpose was the systematic repression of the population. It was hardly surprising, then, that the police paid so little attention to crime; they had other jobs to do.

So far, so fairly normal (for *Al-Lewa*). The next bit was the new departure. This was the sharply personalized form of attacks. There were detailed references to the bizarre, eccentric behaviour of a senior member of the Police Force, culminating recently in open affront to Egyptian womanhood and natural religious feeling (was this part of a deliberate attempt to subvert what had for centuries been the country's orthodox religion?). There were references to the concupiscence of another senior figure, who had for long maintained one whore and who had recently been seen visiting another.

The most detailed reference, however, was to a third (yes, yet another!) even more senior figure whose practices were so blatant that a case he had been involved in had recently been reopened by the Parquet. *Al-Lewa* would not prejudice possible judicial review based on the Parquet's findings but it would venture to suggest that the world would be shocked by the naked political manipulation that would be revealed. At least injuries done to the original native Egyptian incumbents would be exposed.

And that, really, was the point. A perfectly acceptable system had been set aside at the behest of a foreign power. Perfectly capable, decent men had been superseded. What was required was a return to old virtues. Only then would the Police Force be able to lift its head again with pride. But that would require the wholesale and immediate departure of the present holders of office.

'There you are!' said McPhee triumphantly, back in the office. 'A return to the old virtues! Exactly what I've been calling for.'

'And the old personnel,' Owen pointed out.

'Well –'

'That doesn't mean you. It means Mustapha Mir and Philipides.'

'Old virtues!' said Garvin contemptuously. 'Old vices, more like: bribery, corruption, personal favour, brutality, flogging –'

'It's not *Al-Lewa*'s usual line,' said Owen thoughtfully. 'They're a radical paper. They don't usually go for old virtues. They're in favour of new ones.'

'Well, I can see that,' said Garvin. 'That call for efficiency, for instance.'

'I don't think their efficiency is quite the same as yours.'

'Efficiency is efficiency,' said Garvin. 'And, talking of efficiency, how does it come about that they're able to publish something like this? I thought you approved everything beforehand?'

'I didn't this.'

'So how come?'

'They inserted it afterwards.'

'Well, you've got them, then, haven't you?'

'Yes, I've got them. Only –'

'Well, what are you waiting for?'

'I'm surprised. They don't usually carry things this far. They huff and puff and hint and push things just about as far as they think they can go, but they don't usually cross the line. And they don't openly disobey by inserting things afterwards. It's not worth it, you see. They know I'll ban the paper for a spell. They'll lose readers, lose influence. People will read other papers. Their rivals.'

'Radical papers aren't really interested in sales.'

'Don't you kid yourself. They're interested in sales, all right. They want to spread their gospel.'

'So why run the risk by doing this?'

'Why, indeed? It's hardly worth it, is it? Not just for merely another attack on the British.'

'It's not just another attack, though, is it? It's a very specific attack; on us.'

'On all three of us,' said Owen. 'And now I'm beginning to wonder. Maybe the McPhee business is not an isolated event, after all. And maybe, the girl in my bed, the diamond, the necklace, are part of it, too. They're all bound up together; bound up with reopening the Philipides case as well.'

'They're trying to get us out,' said Garvin, 'all three of us. That's the game. That's what it is all about.'

'If that's the game,' said Owen, 'it's a daft one. If we went, the Administration would just put three other Britishers in.'

'*Al-Lewa* would hail it as a triumph.'

'Maybe they would. But I don't think they're behind this. It isn't their sort of thing.'

'Maybe it's about time you found out who *is* behind it,' said Garvin sourly, 'instead of spending all your time drinking coffee in cafés and generally sitting about like a lemon.'

10

Commotion in the Bab-el-Khalk. Cries in the courtyard, activity – unusual, this – in the orderly room. Owen, in his office, heard the agitated slap of slippers coming towards him. It was late in the afternoon and he was the only senior Effendi in the building.

'Effendi, there is a snake in the orderlies' lavatory.'

'Has it bitten someone?'

'No, effendi, but Suleiman wants to use the lavatory.'

'Tell him to use another one. Oh, and send for the snake catcher.'

Doubt.

'Effendi –?'

'Yes?'

'Abdulla is in hospital.'

Abdulla was the usual snake catcher.

'What's wrong with him?'

'He has hurt his back.'

'Send for another.'

'We have, effendi. We sent for Ibrahim and he's not there.'

'Surely there must be someone else? What about my snake catcher? He's a good one.'

'Yes, effendi, but Farouz knows him and says he is visiting his son today.'

'Well, wait a minute, there's one in the Gamaliya. Abu, his name is. Try him.'

Later.

Commotion again.

'What the hell is it this time?'

'Effendi, he's sent a woman.'

'What woman? Oh, Jalila. She's all right. What's the matter?'

'She's a woman, effendi.'

'Yes, I know that.'

'It wouldn't be proper.'

'Does it matter? As long as she gets rid of the snake?'

'Oh, yes, effendi' – chorus – 'it wouldn't be right at all.'

'Why not?'

'What would a woman know about it? Catching snakes is a man's job.'

'She can do it. I've seen her.'

'Yes, but –'

'She would be frightened, effendi.'

'No, she wouldn't. I've seen her get into a tank of snakes.'

'She might get hurt.'

'No, she wouldn't. I've seen her, I tell you. She knows all about it.'

'Effendi –'

He decided he'd better go down. It was indeed Jalila. She was looking defiant.

'I can do it,' she said. 'I often help my father.'

'Helping is one thing, doing another.'

'Why can't he come himself?' asked Owen.

'He's – he's not well.'

'He's dead drunk,' said one of the orderlies.

'He can't come. He's sent me.'

'He doesn't know anything about it.'

'Effendi,' appealed Jalila desperately, 'we need the money.'

'The Rifa'i wouldn't like it,' an orderly said.

Owen thought that was probably true.

'Is he really drunk?' he asked Jalila.

Jalila hung her head.

'Yes, effendi,' she said miserably. 'He always is these days.'

'It's shame,' said one of the orderlies. 'Shame at having a daughter like this.'

Jalila looked at him savagely.

'Can't he be woken up?'

'No, effendi,' said Jalila sadly. 'When he's like this he sleeps for a day and a night.'

'Perhaps we'd better leave it till tomorrow,' said Owen.

'Effendi, Suleiman —'

'You can't have it both ways,' Owen snapped. 'If you won't let her do it, you'll just have to manage without.'

'It would be all right if her father was here,' someone muttered. 'No one minds her helping.'

Owen suddenly had an idea.

'Very well. Fetch him!'

'Fetch him?'

'Carry him if necessary.'

Abu was fetched. He arrived slung unceremoniously across a donkey and snoring loudly.

'Right. Put him down.'

Abu was dumped in the courtyard. Owen bent over him. The stench of alcohol rose up and hit him in the nose.

'He's out for the count, all right,' he said.

'Effendi,' said Jalila in despair, 'believe me, he won't wake up —'

'Never mind that. You get on with it.'

'Get on with it?'

'He's here, isn't he? Right, well, you're helping.'

Jalila looked at him doubtfully.

'Go on. Get on with it.'

Jalila picked up her bag and set out across the yard to the little, square mud-brick building which was the orderlies' lavatory.

The orderlies watched interestedly.

'Rather her than me.'

'It's fortunate it's only a woman.'

Beside the lavatory was a heap of rags which got up as Jalila approached.

141

'Who's that?' said Owen.

'Nassem. He cleans the lavatory.'

Jalila spoke to him and they went round to the back of the lavatory. A moment later Jalila reappeared following a trail which led to a hole in the large whitewashed wall which surrounded the courtyard. On the other side was a piece of wasteland. Owen, guiltily, was reminded of his garden.

Jalila put her bag down and stood for a moment looking around her carefully. A large crowd had gathered, most of them orderlies from within the building, in the hope of seeing something interesting, like the hunt going wrong.

Jalila's eye lit on a small heap of crumbled masonry. She approached it carefully and then squatted down to think. Owen could see what the problem was. The snake was down the hole under the masonry and Jalila couldn't get at its tail. Snake catchers liked to approach from the rear and seize the tail. That way it couldn't twine round something and hold fast.

Jalila went back to her bag, put her hand in and pulled out a snake. She held it for a moment or two in her hand, stroking the back of its head gently with her finger. Then she put it down on the ground in front of the hole. It found a warm brick and settled itself comfortably in the sun.

Nothing happened for about a quarter of an hour. Then something stirred in the hole. A little dark head appeared. It hung there uncertainly for a moment or two and then slid out.

When the snake's whole body was clear of the hole, Jalila pounced, pinning it to the ground with her stick. It tried to rear but couldn't. The head lifted and spat.

Still pinning it with one hand, Jalila dangled a fold of her skirt in front of its face. The snake struck at it savagely, then withdrew its head and struck again. As it lifted its head back, Owen could see the yellow drops on the cloth.

Jalila teased it again, and then again. The snake went on striking until it was exhausted.

'The bag,' said Jalila, 'bring me the bag.'

Owen pushed it towards her. She opened it with one hand and then, quick as a flash, dropped the stick, seized the snake with two hands, lifted it and dropped it in, closing the neck of the bag quickly. For a moment the bag thrashed about. Then it went still.

Unhurriedly, Jalila picked up the other snake, still drowsy about the brick, and dropped that in as well. Then she tied the neck of the bag.

'Well, that was rather disappointing,' said one of the orderlies.

'It all looked a bit easy to me,' said another.

'I don't think the snake was really trying. Probably knew it was a woman.'

'Yes, you get more excitement with a man.'

'Ah, well, that's because snake catching's not really a job for a woman.'

'Lucky her father was here.'

'Back inside!' said Owen. 'All of you. The fantasia is over for the day.'

He paid Jalila generously.

'What about your father?'

Jalila shrugged.

'He can lie there until he comes to,' she said. 'He won't know where he is but that's no different from any other time.'

'You were very good,' said Owen. 'It's harder when you can't see their tails.'

Jalila was pleased and went off beaming.

That evening, as he came out of the Bab-el-Khalk, she was waiting for him.

'I want to thank you,' she said. 'They wouldn't have accepted it if you hadn't made them.'

'I had seen you with snakes,' he said. 'Remember?'

She fell in beside him shyly.

'Yes,' she said. 'That – that is what I wanted to talk to you about.'

In fact, for some time she didn't say anything. As they passed a sherbet shop, Owen considered buying her a sherbet. It was, of course, a thing you did not do; but then, you didn't walk down the street with stray young women, either, not unless they were very stray. Jalila, admittedly, was walking a step behind him, to keep things decent. The position was doubly respectable, since it was a little out to one side, where a suppliant might walk. A wife would walk directly behind. The darkness, however, was probably the greatest safeguard of Jalila's reputation.

'You were kind to me,' she said suddenly, 'so I will help you. You asked me once if I saw the men who had taken the Bimbashi. I did not, but –'

'Yes?'

'I smelt them.'

'What do you mean?'

'In the cistern. There was a smell.'

Owen tried to remember.

'There was a smell of snake?' he said.

'More.'

'Spices,' he said. 'Palm oil.'

He had a very acute sense of smell, which was not always an advantage in Egypt. He tried to conjure back the smells in the cistern. The air had been trapped, he had smelt something distinctly. Snake, he could remember, anyone who had ever kept a snake, even a humble grass snake, knew how the smell clung to your hands, and there in the cistern the smell – sour, acid – had been very pronounced. But what else?

She held out her arm to him.

'Smell,' she said.

It brought back to him the smells in the cistern, pungent, spicy.

'Ointment,' she said. 'You make it from snake fat. Snake fat is the base and then you add to it various spices and other oils. But the main thing is the venom.'

144

'It contains venom?'

'Venom of cobra. You also take it internally. There is a drink called *teryaq*, where the venom is mixed with the juice and rind of limes. You take it in small, very small quantities, but you take it every day.'

'It gives you protection?'

'So they say.'

'And your father has been giving it to you?'

'Yes. But he is not supposed to. It is for the Rifa'i only.'

'But, Jalila,' said Owen, thinking, 'I do not understand. You say you smelt the men?'

'Yes.'

'And this was the smell?'

'Yes. I smelt it in the cistern. The air holds the smell. I knew at once that someone else had been there.'

'But, Jalila, you yourself –'

'I know. But this was different. You see – I should not tell you, it is a secret, it belongs to the Rifa'i – the Rifa'i take it every year. Both the drink and the ointment. They go away for a month – that is where your own snake catcher is, he is not visiting his son, that was just an excuse – they go away for a month, and they take the ointment and the drink every day for a week, and then they have to lie and see there are no ill effects. And they work on things of the spirit. Then they come back ready to do their work. And after they come back, for a week or two the smell is fresh, and –'

'And that was the smell you smelt?'

'Yes.'

'Fresh?'

She nodded.

'My own smell, it is not fresh, because my father, he does not do it properly. He does not know the exercises. He only knows how to prepare the ointment and the *teryaq*. I wear the ointment all the time, the drink I take three times a year.'

'That is too much.'

'I take it in very small doses. A Rifa'i takes a thimbleful. I just cover the bottom of the thimble.'

'And in the cistern it was – not your smell?'

'It was fresh.'

'Whoever it was had been treated recently?'

'Within the last two weeks.'

'And was a snake catcher?'

'One of the Rifa'i. Yes, effendi.'

'You needn't worry about Demerdash,' Zeinab said. 'At least, not about his marrying me. He thinks I'm a whore.'

'Whence has sprung this revelation?'

'He read it in the newspaper.'

'*Al-Lewa*?'

Zeinab nodded.

'I'm sorry.'

'One whore I can cope with,' said Zeinab, 'especially if it happens to be me. It's the other one I'm worried about.'

'There isn't another one.'

'What about the one in your bed?'

'That's the same one, I think.'

'Only this time it was *her* bed?'

'Not even her *appartement*. She wanted to meet me.'

'She certainly believes in making her meetings interesting. I suppose you will tell me you went there in the cause of duty?'

'Of work, yes. She's the wife of the man I told you about; that Greek, Philipides.'

'Isn't one man enough for her?'

'She wanted to intercede for him.'

'You swallowed *that*?'

Owen hesitated.

'I'm not sure. She seemed very passionate.' This, unfortunately, was a singularly ill-chosen word and it was some time before Zeinab could be persuaded to calm down.

'It's me they're after,' he said eventually. 'It's just that you're tied to me, for better or for worse. And, talking of for better or for worse –'

Zeinab always liked him asking her to marry him. It was reassuring; and although she remained in a state of chronic indecision about her answer, considering the matter was very agreeable and tended to put her into a softer mood.

'At least,' she said kindly, 'the competition has now been reduced.'

'Demerdash, you mean?'

'Yes. If there ever was a suit, it has now been withdrawn. He has denounced me to my father.'

'What's it got to do with him?'

'A lot, he thinks. He is concerned about the possible damage to my father's reputation. In fact, he's rather more concerned about that than he is about the damage to mine.'

'Your father's reputation is a matter for your father, I would have thought.'

'Well, no. Not if he is to return to the political fold. Not if he is to be seen as a member of the "Government-in-Waiting".'

'Government-in-Waiting?'

'That's how Demerdash sees it, apparently. Things have reached such a pretty pass, he says, immorality and materialism everywhere, that it's only a question of time before the Khedive dismisses his existing Ministers and looks around him for new ones who can regenerate the country. And when he looks, who will he see? A group of dedicated, experienced men, whose loyalty he can count on, men in whom the country will have confidence, men of standing, Pashas –'

'Pashas?'

'Yes. None of this nonsense about democracy. That's where it all went wrong, when politicians started thinking of themselves as professionals and everyone else started thinking of themselves as politicians. It opened the gates of self-interest. Statesmen, though, are not politicians. They are above all that. Their concern is only for their country –'

'Your father? Demerdash?' said Owen incredulously.

'And the Khedive. What is wanted is a return to the old order, the old ways of doing things, the way it was before the British got here and the Nationalists started uprising, before all the rot set in.'

'And your father believes all *that*?'

'Of course not. But – he's a politician, or was a politician, and, once a politician always a politician. You're always awaiting, if not exactly expecting, the call. Who knows? It could come again. And if it does, he doesn't want to be left out.'

'So he listens to Demerdash?'

'Let's say he's more concerned about my morals than you might think.'

'But, damn it, he's hardly in a position himself –'

'It's one thing for men, another for women. And how can he appear a pillar of the old virtues if his daughter –?'

'Old virtues?' said Owen. 'Old virtues?'

Selim's bulk filled the doorway.

'Effendi –'

'Oh, it's you. Come in. You wanted to see me, I gather?'

'Yes, effendi. It's, well, it's a private matter. I – I wish to ask a favour.'

'Ask away.'

'Effendi, one of my wives has just had a baby.'

'Oh, congratulations! Very pleased to hear it. Not – that wouldn't be Aisha, of course.'

'No, effendi.'

'Leila, was it? But I thought –?'

'No, no, effendi, not Leila either. Fatima.'

'I don't think I've heard about her.'

'Well, no, effendi, with the baby coming, you understand –'

'Quite so. Not so central in your life.'

'Exactly, effendi!' Selim beamed. 'But now the baby's come –'

'Well, very pleased to hear it. Pass on my congratulations, will you?'

'I will indeed, effendi. Effendi, I was wondering –'

'Yes?'

'Well, it was Aisha who put it in my head. She said: "The Effendi has shown you favour. Ask him if he will extend it to the child."'

'Well, of course –'

'If you could come to the seventh day naming, that would be a great honour.'

'A pleasure.'

'Abdul will bring you to my house, effendi. It will only be a small affair, since the child is a girl –'

'A girl? Oh dear! Well, better luck next time.'

'This is the third time. All girls. If she doesn't do better with the fourth,' said Selim darkly, 'she'll have to go.'

'Oh, well, yes. Perhaps you'd better give it a break before trying again?'

'Aisha says we should consult the Aalima. I don't believe in these things myself, especially after all that nonsense about casting out a devil. All the same, it might be worth trying. It's a woman's thing, unfortunately, so you've got to go along with them.'

'Hmm, yes, well –'

It transpired that McPhee had also been invited. This was normal, as McPhee was Selim's direct boss – Owen borrowed constables when he needed them – and it was the practice in the Bab-el-Khalk for superiors to be invited to family festivities. Owen had been to many weddings and several circumcisions but never to a *suboah*, or seventh day naming.

'A most interesting occasion,' said McPhee happily. 'Pre-Muslim and even pre-Christian, I would say. Some resemblance to the Eleusinian rites. Definitely Greek influence. The strewing of flowers – Demeter? Persephone, perhaps? Anyway, definitely Greek.'

'Again?'

'Well,' said McPhee defensively, 'Egypt is a country of mixed cultures and that goes back a long time. Popular ritual is rarely pure, you know. It contains a mixture of elements, incorporates contributions from different cultures. In a place like Egypt, that's a good thing. It brings cultures together, blurs the differences between them. That's half the trouble with the country. As the old popular rituals decay, there's nothing to bring the different groups together, not in a sort of lived celebratory way. So they come apart.'

'There's some sense in that,' said Owen, 'but there's no going back now.'

'But do we have to go onwards quite so fast?' asked McPhee. 'It sometimes seems to me that the aspirations of the politicians – and of the people like Garvin who are always wanting to change things – are running ahead of what ordinary people actually want.'

'Yes, well,' said Owen. 'See you there!'

Back in his office. Selim again.

'Effendi, it's not my idea,' said Selim, 'it's hers.'

'What idea?'

'To invite the Aalima. We need someone to preside at the ceremony and Aisha said why not try the Aalima? Effendi, I'm not too happy about this, mine has always been a respectable house, well, fairly respectable, and I said, what with the Effendi coming, not to mention the Bimbashi, I mean, what would the Bimbashi think, he might think someone was going to slip something in his drink, but, effendi, there won't be anything like that, I mean, there *will* be something in the drink, but just for you and me, I'll see to that, anyway, Aisha said why not *ask* the Effendi instead of just saying no – so would you mind, effendi?' concluded Selim, looking at Owen anxiously.

'Mind?' said Owen. 'No I don't think so. No,' he said, 'I don't think so at all.'

*　　　*　　　*

As Owen was passing the orderly room, he bumped into the orderly from whom McPhee had first heard about the Zzarr.

'Greetings, Osman,' he said heartily. 'How is your cousin?'

'Cousin?' said the orderly unhappily.

'Amina, I think her name was. Or wasn't.'

'She is well,' Osman muttered.

'Good. And have you given back the hundred piastres, as you said you would?'

'Not yet, effendi,' the orderly admitted. 'I have not seen the man –'

'A pity. I was hoping you were keeping an eye open for him.'

'I am, effendi, oh, I am!'

'I hope you see him soon.'

Osman looked despondent.

'And what did Zeinab think?' asked Mahmoud.

'She wondered who the other whore was.'

Mahmoud laughed, but uncomfortably. It was exactly her capacity to make this kind of remark that bothered him about Zeinab. He wasn't quite sure how to handle it, coming from a woman. Mahmoud, like most young Egyptians of the professional classes, had had very few opportunities of meeting women at all; still less one of the 'new' European sort. In theory, he approved of female emancipation; encountering it in practice, however, made him uncomfortable. And then there was this business of sexual liberation. Again, in principle, Mahmoud was all in favour; in practice he felt uncomfortable about the relationship between Owen and Zeinab.

'You may be interested, too.'

'Well, I think –' began Mahmoud, even more uncomfortably.

'Mrs Philipides.'

Mahmoud shot bolt upright in his chair.

'*Our* Mrs Philipides?'

Owen nodded.

'The same.'

'But –'

He told Mahmoud about his encounters with the lady.

'But this is wrong!' said Mahmoud. 'Very wrong! Trying to influence the course of justice by favours. Bribery and – and sexual favours!'

'She seemed to think that was the way to proceed.'

'Well, I know that has been the practice in the past. But – but we're trying to get away from it now. It's outrageous!'

'As you say, it's the old way of doing things. Which Garvin, of course, is trying to change. And *Al-Lewa*, it appears, is anxious to go back to.'

'That is a mistake!' cried Mahmoud. 'They are quite mistaken. I assure you, that is not the position of the Nationalist Party. It is precisely that sort of thing that we wish to get rid of. It is humiliating, shaming!'

He banged his fist on the table.

'In this case,' said Owen, 'it is also puzzling. Why does she address me?'

'You're the Mamur Zapt.'

'Yes, but you're in charge of the investigation. Why doesn't she solicit you?'

'Because she knows I wouldn't –'

'Thank you.'

Mahmoud beat his brow with his fists.

'What have I said? Forgive me, dear friend, forgive me!'

He leaped up and embraced Owen. 'I withdraw that! I withdraw that absolutely!'

He sat down again and buried his face in his hands. The people at adjoining tables did not even look up. They took this as perfectly normal conversational behaviour.

'Actually,' said Owen, 'I don't think it's that, or just that. Or even that she's so locked in the past that she thinks the Mamur Zapt is still the one to go to. I wonder, in fact, if this is about intercession at all.'

Mahmoud raised his head and stared.

'Well, of course it is!' he said. 'It must be. What else?'

'There were three of us attacked in that article,' said Owen, 'and I wonder if it is just coincidence.'

'I don't understand.'

'I am wondering whether the Philipides business connects up with the McPhee business. Not to mention the side-swipes aimed at me.'

'But how could – I mean, why should –?'

'I wonder if there is a plot to get rid of the three of us.'

'Oh, my dear fellow,' said Mahmoud, putting a hand on Owen's arm, 'how could there be? It is so unlikely!'

'Any more unlikely,' said Owen, 'than that Garvin should have tried to get rid of Mustapha Mir, Philipides and Wainwright?'

Georgiades came into the office and perched himself on Nikos's desk, which he knew Nikos hated. It was not that Nikos had anything personal against Georgiades; it was just that, obsessively tidy-minded, he believed that the top of a desk was for paper not flesh.

'That orderly of Philipides,' Georgiades said. 'Hassan was his name; you were going to go through the lists.'

'Halfway through,' said Nikos, without raising his head.

'Don't bother. He's not dead.'

'Right!' said Nikos, without interest.

'Not dead?' said Owen, overhearing.

'No. Alive and kicking. And in the Gamaliya somewhere. I've found someone who knows him. Would you like to meet him?'

11

The *kahweh* was like any other coffee shop which you might find in the poorer, more traditional quarters. Along its front was a raised stone seat, or *mastaba*, about three feet high and about the same width. Similar benches ran along the walls of the single room inside. They were the only seats. You sat with your back against the wall and, if you smoked, your pipe on the ground beside you.

In this hot weather most of the customers had brought their water pipes. There was a gourd-shaped bowl on the ground which held the water and the smoke was inhaled through a flexible hose. The whole contraption was quite a thing to carry and if you were sick you employed a servant for that purpose. Most of the men of the *kahweh* were not rich and carried their own.

Owen and Georgiades stepped down into the room inside. For a moment they stopped to let their eyes grow accustomed to the dark. The only light came through the open front door. In this country the object was to keep the sun out, not let it in.

There was hardly anyone inside. Most of the regulars preferred to sit outside on the exterior *mastaba*, where they could take the air and chat with the people going past. That suited Owen and he made for an empty corner on the other side of the room.

Cups were brought first, little porcelain ones held inside larger brass ones which were better for holding. The coffee came in a hanging pot, supported from three chains and with charcoal at the bottom. The strong bitter smell filled the room.

Sayeed Abdullah arrived a few minutes later. He was a small, spare man with the hair at his temples beginning to grey. He walked with a limp.

He greeted them in a way you seldom saw now, putting his hands to his brow and ducking his head. He seemed nervous of their proffered hands and shook them hesitantly. Then he sat down on the *mastaba* beside them tucking one leg up beneath him. The other, the injured one, he let hang.

He had met Georgiades before and for a while, until the man became used to him, Owen was content to let the two make conversation. Talk was mainly about old times. Sayeed Abdullah had been an orderly at one of the sub-police stations in the Citadel quarter. Georgiades appeared to know it well and they had acquaintances in common, most of whom had now retired. Georgiades asked after them.

At last he came to the point, the point that Sayeed had been expecting.

'And Hassan?'

'He still comes.'

'You see him?' asked Owen.

'Every week,' said Sayeed Abdullah. 'He comes round to collect.'

'Collect?' said Owen. 'What is it that he is collecting?'

'The subscription,' said Georgiades.

'Subscription? What to? A benefit society or something?'

'You could call it that.'

'In those days, effendi,' Sayeed Abdullah explained, 'if you wanted a job with the police, you would go to someone who could arrange it. You paid them money, of course. Usually you did not have money. So you would agree to pay so much a week after you got the job.'

'But surely that was years ago? How is it that Hassan is still collecting? You must have paid the debt off years ago.'

'That is what I said, effendi.'

'And?'

Sayeed pointed to his leg.

'He did that?'

'They did that. Effendi, I still would not have paid, only afterwards, when I was in hospital, they came and said: First you, then your wife, then your sons. So I paid.'

'But all this was long ago. You have left the service, Hassan has left –'

'That is why he collects, effendi. He needs the money, he says.'

'Even though you no longer have the job?'

'I have a pension, effendi. It was given me after – after this.'

He touched his leg.

'It must be very small.'

'After I have paid the subscription,' said Sayeed Abdullah, 'there is little left.'

'Why have you not told someone?'

Sayeed Abdullah looked at him steadily.

'Who should I speak to, effendi, seeing for whom Hassan worked?'

'It is different now.'

'So they say.'

'It *is* different now,' said Georgiades.

Sayeed Abdullah shrugged.

'Hassan still comes round,' he said. 'And I still have a wife and sons.'

'Are there others like you?' asked Owen.

'I do not ask, effendi. But I think so.'

'And they, too, were treated like this?'

He pointed to Sayeed's leg.

'After they had seen what happened to me,' said Sayeed Abdullah, 'that was not necessary.'

Owen signalled for more coffee. Sayeed Abdullah acknowledged it with the same old-fashioned, traditional bob of the head as before.

'He had other ways, too,' he said. 'There was a new

man who came to our station. He was just up from the country and had a new wife who was expecting a child. Hassan had a friend, an evil woman who could cast spells. And he said to this man who had come up from the country, if you do not pay, I know someone who will put the evil eye on your wife.'

'And did he pay?'

'No, effendi. He said, what is this nonsense about the evil eye? But the baby died, effendi, and the next time he paid.'

Owen was silent for a while. Then he said: 'It is time this was ended.'

'That was what your friend said.' Sayeed Abdullah looked at Georgiades. 'He said, too, that you were the man who could end it.'

'I need your help.'

'You want me to speak,' said Sayeed Abdullah. 'Yes, I know.'

'And will you?'

'It is easy to ask, effendi. Harder to do, if you have a wife and sons.'

'I shall put Hassan in a place where he will not be able to harm you. And until then I will give you a guard. In fact, I know just the man. For both you and your family.'

Sayeed Abdullah hesitated.

'It is easy for you, effendi. Things happen not to you but to people in the streets.'

'I intend to see that they don't happen to people in the streets. But for that I need your help.'

Sayeed Abdullah sat for a long time looking down on the ground. Then he raised his eyes.

'I will do it, effendi. Because I know that only in this way can it be ended, effendi, I will do as you ask.'

Owen sat there with him until Georgiades returned with the guard he had in mind. Selim.

He noticed the change in atmosphere as soon as he got back to the Bab-el-Khalk. The bearers, who normally

157

greeted him with backchat, averted their eyes. He went into his office and summoned his orderly.

'What's up?'

Yussuf considered beating about the bush, then took a look at Owen's face and decided not to.

'Effendi, you're in trouble.'

'Why?'

'That snake business. Everyone thinks you pulled a fast one. The Rifa'i don't like it.'

'What are they complaining about? We tried to use our ordinary snake catcher, didn't we? And then when we couldn't find him we tried to use others. We couldn't find anybody. They want to make it a bit more possible to find their members before they start complaining.'

'Effendi,' said Yussuf desperately, 'that's not the idea.'

'What do you mean, it's not the idea?'

'It's the other way round. The Rifa'i want to make it harder to find a snake catcher when you want one. That way they can put their prices up.'

'And that's what they were doing?'

'Yes, effendi,' said Yussuf sadly, 'and you spoiled it.'

'Well, that's too bad.'

'Yes, effendi, but now everyone's afraid the Rifa'i will put the snakes back and . . . and . . .'

'Yes?'

'Suleiman wants to use the lavatory again.'

Zeinab had been out having her hair done. She frequented a modish salon in the Ismailiya and used it as an opportunity to catch up with the fashionable gossip of the town. Today she was gleeful.

'The Whore of Babylon!' she said. 'Samira is most envious.'

'What's all this?'

'They've been reading *Al-Lewa*. It is not, it must be confessed, a paper that they usually read but when they heard that I was in it . . . ! "What company you keep, Zeinab", Felicite said; "all those policemen! Still, someone must be the criminal, I suppose.'' And do you know what they say? There's going to be more tomorrow.'

'Oh, is there?' said Owen. 'I'll soon see about that.'

'They don't mind. Demerdash is paying all the fines, you see.'

'Demerdash?'

'Unlikely, I know. And I do take it amiss. Gets the paper to write the article and then blames me for appearing in it!'

'Just a minute. Are you sure?'

'That's what Iolanthe says, and she should know since she's sleeping with Daouad. They can hardly believe their luck, she says, and can only think Demerdash has never read the paper. Well, that's quite possible, I suppose; he's been out of the country a long time and I dare say that in Damascus or Constantinople or wherever he's been he doesn't get much chance to keep up with things. But I do think it's nasty of him to get me put in the paper or, at least, not to object, and then to make all that fuss with my father! Still,' said Zeinab, thinking, 'I prefer that to the other way round.'

'What other way round?' said Owen, lost.

'Denunciation to wooing,' said Zeinab. 'At least, in Demerdash's case.'

'Got another one?' said the snake catcher, looking around Owen's garden. 'They do come thick and fast. It's the heat, I expect.'

'No, it's not a snake this time,' said Owen. 'It's just that I wanted to ask you something.'

'Oh!' said the snake catcher, disappointed, letting his bag drop on the ground.

'Of course, I'll make it worth your while. I know it's your time.'

'Ah, well, that's different!' said the snake catcher, brightening up.

The smell was, as Jalila had said, very distinct, the same as on her own arms but stronger, spicier, fresher.

'I could have done with you the other day,' said Owen.

'That business at the Bab-el-Khalk? Well, you're getting into deep water there, you know.'

'I would have sent for you, only they said you were visiting your son.'

The snake catcher looked vague.

'Yes,' he said. 'I think so.'

'I don't,' said Owen, smiling. He gave an exaggerated sniff. 'Funny smell,' he said.

The snake catcher looked at him guardedly.

'It's once a year you go, isn't it? There's the balsam, of course. And then there's the *teryaq*. And of course, it has to be done in the right way, in the right frame of mind. That's why you need a teacher, I expect.'

'It may be,' said the snake catcher non-committally.

'Well, I'm not going to ask you about it because I know these things are secret. But I want to know the name of your teacher.'

'I can't tell you that!' said the snake catcher, aghast.

'I think you can. The teacher is not secret. It's what he teaches that's secret.'

It took Owen a long time to persuade him. It took a lot of promises and quite a lot of money. But eventually he got what he wanted.

Owen found Mahmoud pacing about his office. He turned an angry face towards him.

'The Khedive's birthday!' he spat out. 'What do I care about the Khedive's birthday?'

'What, indeed?' said Owen, taken aback.

'Look at this!' said Mahmoud, with a fiery gesture towards his desk, piled high with papers. 'I'm in court twice this week, three times next. Five cases to be finalized! How do they think I'm going to do it?'

'Well –'

'There's always a lot of preparation at the last moment. Witnesses to be taken through their evidence, clerks to be chivvied – they always leave things till it's almost too late, damn them. And then something like this happens!'

'What exactly –?'

'You haven't heard? No, and nor has anyone else. And do you know why? Because he only made up his mind to do it this week. This week!'

'Sorry, his birthday, you said? Surely –?'

'Public holiday. He's declared a public holiday for the day after tomorrow.'

'Oh!'

'Yes,' said Mahmoud. 'Exactly!'

He plunged into his chair and buried his face in his hands.

'Lunacy!' he said. 'Sheer lunacy!'

'It's not that bad.'

'It is,' said Mahmoud, refusing to be consoled. 'How can you achieve anything when everything is so – so capricious?'

'Well –'

'It's so *inefficient*!' he burst out in exasperation.

The best thing, Owen knew from long experience of Mahmoud, was to change the subject.

'That Philipides business,' he said; 'how are you getting on?'

'That's an example,' said Mahmoud, declining to be sidetracked. 'Not at all. I've been going through the records to check which police officers were in post at the time; I wanted to ask them what they knew about it, if they'd been approached in the same way as Bakri.'

'And had they?'

'They weren't saying.'

'It's hardly surprising. They might find themselves incriminating their mates. Or even themselves.'

'Yes.' Mahmoud, calm now, sat back in his chair. 'Of course, there's another explanation possible.'

'What's that?'

'That Bakri was the only instance. And that Garvin made the most of it.'

'According to Philipides, there were enough other ones to make Wainwright open an investigation.'

'Not quite. He may have *feared* there were other ones. The only one he may have actually known about was the Bakri case. That's why it's so important to get Wainwright out here. Only then can we know what prompted his action.'

'Bakri said there were others.'

'If you're caught on a thing like this, you usually do.'

'Are you saying there weren't any others? That Bakri was the only one and that Garvin –'

'Made the most of it. For his own ends.'

'You still think it was a plot to get the Egyptians out and the British in?'

'I think it may have been much more localized than it was made out to be at the time. And much less significant.'

'You talked to the police: did you talk to the orderlies?'

'No. Should I?'

'There's a man I would like you to meet.'

'The Khedive's birthday?' said Garvin in tones of disgust. 'Another comic caper we could do without!'

'Oh, I don't know,' protested Owen, who had been looking forward to spending a complete day with Zeinab. 'He can hardly help having a birthday, can he?'

'Yes, but this is his second this year already!'

'Well, it'll be popular.'

'Popular?' said Garvin dourly. 'I hope so. Because the highlight of it is going to be a big parade in front of the Abdin Palace at which my job will be to see that one of those subjects with whom he's so popular doesn't take a pot-shot at him!'

'Keep them at a distance.'

'And put plenty of soldiers between them and him, yes, I know. I tell you,' said Garvin bitterly, 'the amount of money and time wasted on a thing like this is immense.'

He sat down heavily in his chair.

'What was it you were going to ask me?'

'The Philipides business. His orderly was a man named Hassan.'

'Oh. I remember him,' said Garvin. 'A nasty piece of work. He got out just in time. Otherwise he'd have been in the dock along with the others.'

'It may only have been deferred. Can you tell me anything about him?'

'Not much. He was a go-between, the man who put the bite on. There were rumours of violence and coercion. I was sufficiently bothered to put a guard on Bakri.'

'Very wise. Anything else?'

'It's a while ago now,' said Garvin, shaking his head.

'I'm trying to track him down. You've no idea where I might look, have you?'

'Afraid not.'

'He's been seen in the Gamaliya.'

'He used to know that district, certainly. He was at the sub-station there for several years before he moved to the Citadel. I remember, because I checked to see if there was anyone else like Bakri.'

'And was there?'

'If there were,' said Garvin, 'they weren't saying.'

As Owen walked through the city the following day, there were signs of the coming celebrations. Bunting hung across some of the streets and clusters of brightly-coloured balloons dangled from the overhanging windows. Little boys were decorating their sheep before the open doors of their houses.

As soon as he penetrated into the older part, however, the bunting disappeared. In these medieval streets the Khedive was a parvenu. The allegiances they acknowledged were older.

'The sheikh? Certainly, effendi. I will show you.'

'Sheikh' was a courtesy title extended to anyone of venerable years and a reputation for piety or learning. Genuine scholars – Sheikh Musa, for instance – might have challenged this particular application on both counts.

Ordinary people, however, thought it prudent to recognize with respect the peculiar knowledge that the 'sheikh' laid claim to. He was the man who supervised the spiritual exercises of the Rifa'i when they withdrew for their annual period of re-preparation.

'I have heard about you,' said the sheikh. 'You are no friend of the Rifa'i.'

'On the contrary,' said Owen, 'I have come because I am their friend.'

'You are the Mamur Zapt?'

'Yes.'

'The Mamur Zapt is the friend of the great. He can never be the friend of the Rifa'i.'

'Because he is the friend of the great, he can sometimes avert the wrath of the great.'

'Why should the wrath of the great be turned on the Rifa'i?'

'Because one of the Rifa'i has done a bad thing.'

'If he has, then the fault belongs to him and not to the Rifa'i.'

'That is true, and that is what I think, too. And so I am anxious to separate the man from the Rifa'i.'

'How might that be done?'

'It would need your help.'

'Tell me what you want,' said the sheikh, 'and then I will tell you if I will help you.'

'Men come to you for preparation,' said Owen. 'Some have come to you recently. I would like you to give me their names.'

'That is a secret.'

'Think for a moment,' said Owen. 'A snake catcher is known by repute. If I wish, I can find out the names of all the snake catchers in the city. I can find out, too, those that were away at the time. Such knowledge is no secret. I could find it out myself.'

'If you can find it out for yourself,' said the sheikh, 'why ask me?'

'So that I can find out more quickly. Before more harm is done.'

The sheikh considered.

'It is true,' he said after a while, 'that there are bad men among the Rifa'i.'

'Let us separate the two,' said Owen, 'so that I look at the men and not at the Rifa'i.'

The sheikh regarded him thoughtfully.

'The Khedive's birthday!' said McPhee the next day. 'Splendid!'

The parade had passed off without anyone taking a pot-shot at their sovereign. The reception, held safe behind the iron railings of the palace, had been undergone. The Khedive had at last retired thankfully to his private apartments; and everybody else had taken to the streets.

By the time Owen emerged from the palace, the Midan was full of little stalls. There were two sorts of stall. There were the ones in which the well-to-do sat and consumed Turkish delight or sherbet. These were carpeted enclosures; only the carpets were on the walls not on the floor. The walls were about four feet high so that those inside could see and be seen.

The other sort of stall was the ordinary selling stall which normally blocked most of Cairo's streets. Usually they sold vegetables. Today they sold sweets, a source of friction between them and the ordinary sweetmeat vendors. Cairo had a sweet tooth and the chief point of occasions like this, it seemed, was to indulge it. For the very poorest there were sticks of sugar cane, to be sucked with audible gusto. Even a few milliemes, however, would purchase a bag of boiled or a jar of jellied or, more likely, a shapeless, sticky, multi-coloured mess of mucked about sugar. Young, old, Copt, Arab, Greek, Turk, Albanian, Montenegrin, all in their best boots and traditional finery, walked up and down among the stalls guzzling sweets.

'Splendid!' said McPhee, with deep satisfaction.

'They could be doing worse things, I suppose,' said Owen. 'Killing each other, for example.'

'In a country like Egypt,' said McPhee seriously, 'where there is so much ethnic and religious tension, it is important to relieve the tensions occasionally.'

'By eating sweets?'

'Well –'

'A country glued together with sugar?'

'You may scoff, Owen, but traditional festivity serves a purpose and does more for social order than any amount of efficiency in the Police Force.'

'Hello!' said Garvin, coming up beside them.

'Oh, hello. We were just talking about efficiency.'

Garvin looked a little surprised.

'Well,' he said, 'it didn't go off too badly, I must admit. I brought the band forward and that screened off one side. It was a good idea, don't you think?'

'Oh, very good.'

McPhee slipped off. Garvin and Owen strolled down between the lines of stalls.

Suddenly Garvin ducked away. Owen pushed after him and found him standing over an old, scantily-dressed Arab, from the Western deserts, it looked, who was squatting beside a pile of twigs. As Owen looked, Garvin picked up a twig and put the end in his mouth.

'Haven't had any of this since, oh, eighteen ninety-seven,' he said happily, 'when I was in the Desert Patrol.'

'What is it?'

'A kind of liquorice root. Try some.'

Owen declined and left Garvin chatting away to the old Arab. One of the disconcerting things about Garvin was that when he could remember to forget about efficiency he actually knew quite a lot about Egypt.

He caught up with McPhee.

'I'll give you an example,' said McPhee, harking back to their previous conversation, on which he had evidently been brooding. 'I'm sure the C-G shouldn't have been so cavalier over the Molid-en-Nebbi.'

'Things were getting out of hand.'

One of the highlights of the Molid-en-Nebbi, the Birth-day of the Prophet, had been for the devoted to lie down in the street in scores so that the Descendant of the Prophet could ride over them. The British, possibly con-cerned about the risk to the horses, had decreed that the practice should no longer continue.

'Or take the Ashura as an example.'

'Well, yes, take the Ashura.'

One of the features of the Ashura procession was that it was preceded by hundreds of dervishes slashing them-selves with knives and scourging their bare backs with chains.

Banned, too.

'Well, I don't know –' McPhee began.

'I do,' said Mahmoud, who had just joined them. 'It is a disgusting practice.'

'Centuries old!'

'Time it was stopped. What impression of us do you think it gives to tourists? That we go in for self-mutilation?'

'Incidental,' said McPhee. 'Incidental.'

Owen fell in beside Mahmoud and they drifted away together.

'How is it that you're here?' asked Owen. 'Joining them if you can't beat them?'

'Passing through,' said Mahmoud. 'I've just been at a big meeting at the Ecole de Droit.'

Owen didn't ask after the nature of the meeting, but if it had been timed so as to clash with the festivities it was unlikely to be a gathering of supporters of the regime, and if it was being held in the Law School, it was almost cer-tainly a Nationalist meeting of some sort.

'The trouble with festivities,' said Mahmoud, 'is that they are a kind of popular obscurantism.'

Owen was still trying to work out what this meant when he saw Garvin directly ahead of them. He wondered for a moment if he should pilot Mahmoud the other way. It was too late; they were on him.

They greeted each other with reserve, but politely.

'Mahmoud was just saying that all this is a kind of popular obscurantism.'

Garvin understood the point in a flash.

'Distracts from the struggle, does it?'

'It's the circus that goes with the bread,' said Mahmoud.

'McPhee would disagree with you,' said Owen. 'He believes that the sugar sweetens the tensions.'

'That's the same point,' said Garvin.

'And dissolves them.'

'Well –'

Garvin and Mahmoud looked at each other and laughed and walked on beside each other for a little while. Owen got held up by a camel. When he caught up with them they were deep in conversation.

'The *second* time he's done it,' said Garvin. 'Twice in a year!'

'Well, yes. I suppose with all the preparation –'

'Exactly. But it knocks on all the way back. Government offices –'

'The Courts –'

'Firms.'

'Business.'

'He just doesn't realize.'

'It's the *time*!'

'The inefficiency!'

'Yes,' said Mahmoud, slightly surprised, 'the inefficiency.'

12

Owen, who had long ago learned that the only way of being sure, in Egypt, especially in hot weather, that a thing had been done was to go yourself and see it had been done, paid a visit to the household of Sayeed Abdullah. It was in a tiny street below the Citadel, right on the edge of the city. The houses here were single-storey, simple blocks with flat roofs. Some of them had tiny yards, in which the people did their cooking and as Owen went past he caught the wafts of fried onions. It was about the time of the evening meal, when it was still light enough to see but darkness was beginning to take the heat out of the air.

He found the house and knocked on the door. Somebody moved on the roof above him. Perhaps the family was already up there, where later they would spread the beds and sleep, trying to catch a breath of evening air. After a moment, as no one came, he stepped back to call up.

And then someone came round the side of the building, out of the shadows and put him in an expert neck-lock.

He immediately raised both his feet off the ground and then drove the heels of his shoes hard down the front of the bare shins of his assailant. The man gasped and involuntarily released the lock just enough to allow Owen to drive back with his elbow. He twisted round and broke loose enough to free the other arm. He brought his fist in hard but it was partially blocked and thudded into the shoulder, rather than against the neck as he had intended.

He didn't get a second chance but was at once enveloped in an enormous bear hug. His feet were lifted right off the ground and he was swung round and crashed against the wall.

Every bit of breath was jolted out of him. His attacker prepared to swing again. Owen couldn't stop him and had to take the blow. This time, though, he was able to raise his feet behind him, put them against the wall, and push off. His attacker, still holding him fast, staggered back across the street. They came out into some lamplight.

'Why, effendi!' said the surprised voice of Selim.

The mighty grip loosened.

'Jesus!' said Owen. 'What's going on?'

'You told me, effendi!'

'I just said, guard him!'

'You said no one was to get at him!'

'Yes, but I didn't say kill anyone who approached!'

He was able to speak now and his head had not been torn off as at first he supposed. He was even able to reflect that at least Selim was obeying instructions effectively.

'Sorry, effendi,' said Selim contritely.

'It's OK. You were quite right,' said Owen grudgingly. 'Best to be on the safe side.'

'Sayeed has told me they are bad men, effendi,' Selim explained, 'so I thought it best to strike first and caution afterwards.'

'In this instance,' said Owen, 'you are probably right.'

'Nasty bastards,' said Selim, leading Owen into the house. 'Did you see what they did to his leg? I've promised him that if I get the chance, I'll do the same to them. You needn't worry though, effendi, they'll still be able to talk afterwards. Just.'

Selim, it transpired, was already a great favourite of the family. He and Abdul covered the guard duty in shifts. Since, when they were not assaulting astonished visitors, the duty entailed staying indoors in the shade, drinking innumerable cups of tea and spending most of the time chatting to Sayeed, they embraced their responsibilities with relish.

'We are beloved of the family,' Selim assured him.

Not too beloved, Owen hoped, and had a private word with Selim about this before he left.

'Effendi,' swore Selim, 'I will not lay a finger upon her. You can rely on me. Especially as she is old enough to be my grandmother.'

Even so, Owen had his doubts. As to Selim's discharge of the rest of his duties, he was, on reflection, rather more satisfied. A little over-enthusiastic, perhaps, but on the whole Owen thought it best not to complicate matters by urging moderation in other things as well.

The expected newspaper attacks appeared. They were aimed this time, however, chiefly at Owen. 'Why me?' he complained to Paul.

'They must think you're getting somewhere,' suggested Paul. 'Of course, they're not very well informed.'

Owen had gone to the lengths of calling on Paul in his office at the Consulate-General.

'Not because you're bothered about newspaper attacks,' said Paul.

'Them? Oh no, it's something else.' He hesitated. 'Actually, I do feel I might be getting somewhere. Only I'm not going to do it in time. Before Wainwright gets here. Or, at least, before he leaves England in order to get here. In which case it will be too late to stop him.'

'He will be leaving England the day after tomorrow,' said Paul.

'You don't think – if he could just be delayed a little?'

'Tried that,' said Paul, 'but he wants to get out in time for the Flower Show.'

He was, however, thinking. Suddenly, he squared his shoulders.

'I have a duty,' he said. 'A duty to obstruct anyone who goes to a Flower Show other than by accident. I will try again. This time I will raise my game.'

He took a pad of Governmental telegram forms from a drawer in his desk and picked up a pen. A few minutes later he stopped and rang his bell. A worried middle-aged man appeared.

'Wilson, what do gardeners do in the garden in England at this time of the year?'

'Not much.'

'They must do something. My mother is always out there.'

'Dig?'

'Something technical.'

'Water dahlias?'

'That will do nicely. Thank you, Wilson.'

When he had finished, he passed the result to Owen.

'How's that?'

Consul General to Wainwright

Deeply grieve to inform you Flower Show cancelled.

'Paul,' said Owen, 'it's not been cancelled!'

'Think he'll check?'

He picked up the pen and made an alteration.

Flower Show likely postponed.

'Paul,' said Owen, 'won't he check that too?'

'Ah, yes, but I'll get the Old Man to ask the Committee if it *ought* to be postponed. In view of the heat. They'll argue about it for days and by the time they've made up their minds it'll be too late to do anything other than postpone it.'

'He may wonder why it's postponed.'

'The heat. I'll put that in.'

Postponed due to extreme heat. Likewise judicial investigation.

'Paul, do you think that'll convince him? I mean, he's been out here, he knows about the heat.'

'Should I make it stronger? Perhaps: Due to extreme heat and political unrest.'

'*The Flower Show*? Postponed because of political unrest?'

'Certainly. There's always political unrest about Flower Shows. My mother –'

'Paul, that's in the Cotswolds. In England.'

'All right. I'll make it clear that it's the inquiry that might be affected by political unrest. How about this?'

Deeply grieve to inform you Flower Show postponement due extreme heat. In view judicial inquiry also likely postponed political unrest suggest delay departure. Will inform you when situation changes. Further consideration your part: danger dahlias.

McPhee and Owen arrived together. Selim met them beaming and ushered them at once into the small yard. Every inch was decorated with bunting and the air was heavy with the scent of sweet peas, huge bunches of which were scattered everywhere. Along one side of the wall was a low table on which stood vast bowls of hot rice and buttered beans.

'Heavens!' said Owen. 'How many are you expecting?'

'No one, effendi,' said Selim, with a broad flash of white teeth.

This was, as McPhee pointed out, the correct ritual answer. In theory, namings were modest domestic occasions, kept deliberately low-key in order to avert the wrath of malign spirits which might envy the good fortune of the family if too ostentatious a display was made. In practice, of course, no one could resist the chance of a binge and Selim had invited the whole street.

Plus a few more. Owen recognized many faces from the Bab-el-Khalk, together with those of constables and orderlies from many of the city's sub-stations. He had also noticed Sayeed Abdullah, who greeted Owen with his usual deferential bob of the head.

'Well, I couldn't leave the poor old chap at home by himself, could I?' Selim excused himself.

'What about the family?' said Owen, a trifle anxiously.

'Oh, they're here too,' Selim assured him. 'Inside.'

Which was where, for the moment, all the women were. If there were as many of them as there were of men in the yard there were more than a hundred in the tiny, two-room house. Owen could not believe that to be possible. Mother and baby, of course, were inside, too.

'How's the baby?' he asked, again with some anxiety.

'Baby?' said Selim, a little vaguely. 'Oh, yes, baby. Oh, very well, very well.'

He showed Owen and McPhee up to the place of honour on the roof. Two rickety cane chairs had been placed on the very edge, where there was a good view down into the yard.

Selim clapped his hands.

'Beans for the Effendis! And lemonade. *Good* lemonade,' he whispered to Owen with a nudge.

'Not for the Bimbashi,' Owen whispered back.

'Not this time, no,' said Selim, with a great laugh.

The lemonade, in Owen's case, turned out to be marissa beer. He sipped it contentedly and looked down on the spectacle below.

'Where's that bitch of an Aalima?' said Selim crossly.

Down in the street there was a thunderous knocking. A little later the Aalima appeared. She went round the yard sprinkling something on the ground.

'Fennel and maize,' said McPhee, 'the fruits of the earth. Fertility symbols, obviously. And salt.'

'Salt?'

'To avert the evil eye. That's what she's singing. "Salt in the eye of the evil beholder."'

'Is she doing that right?' asked Selim anxiously.

'Oh, I think so.'

'If she's not,' said Selim, still only half-convinced, 'I'll put some salt on her tail all right.'

'No, no,' said McPhee, 'she knows her stuff.'

'It's just that after what Sayeed said –'

'What was that?' said Owen. 'What did Sayeed say?'

'About the evil eye,' said Selim. 'We don't want any of that here.'

'Ssh –!' whispered McPhee. 'This is the important bit.'

The baby was brought out into the yard. First it was paraded round the yard to general appreciation. Then it was given to its mother, who had now appeared in the yard and was seated on a special chair festooned with flowers and coloured handkerchiefs. An older woman brought out a brass mortar which she put right next to the baby's head and then struck repeatedly with a pestle.

'That's so that it doesn't grow up to be frightened of mirth and music,' said McPhee.

Finally, the child was placed in what looked to Owen very like an ordinary sieve and shaken.

'What's that? A sieve?'

'It's to prevent tummy upsets,' said McPhee.

The baby survived these and other ordeals and then was brought up to the roof for presentation to Owen and McPhee.

Owen knew, at least, about this bit and produced some coins, which the baby's mother tied into its hair.

Everyone waited expectantly.

'What is its name going to be?' whispered McPhee.

'Name?'

'Mahbuba,' whispered Selim.

'Fatima,' whispered his wife.

Selim glared at her.

'Khadija,' said Owen, 'Khadija Mahbuba Fatima,' and hoped that everyone was satisfied.

'Well, that's that,' said Selim. 'Now, perhaps, we can get on with things.'

Owen asked if the baby and mother would like to stay on the roof in the cool air.

'Stay on the roof?' said Selim, astonished. 'The place for them is indoors. *I'm* on the roof.'

Baby and mother disappeared below.

'Lemonade?' said Selim happily. 'There's plenty. Don't hold back!'

For some time a set of bagpipes had been trying without success to push its way into the densely-packed yard. At last someone saw it.

'The musicians! God be praised! The musicians have arrived.'

A way was not exactly cleared but found: bagpipes and man were hoisted into the air and passed over the heads of the crowd until they reached the opposite wall, where the bagpipes player established a perch for himself. He was shortly joined by two drummers and a cymbals player, transported likewise. With a roll on the drums the music began.

Down in the yard, men began to writhe. That was about all there was room for. It soon became evident, however, that some men could writhe better than others and it was not long before they attracted a certain space and following. Women now began to appear in the doorways and at the edge of the yard, watching admiringly. Whatever might be the case in the houses of the rich, where troupes of female gipsy *Ghawazi* dancers might be hired for the occasion, in more lowly houses it was the men who danced.

Selim, monarch for the moment of all he surveyed, was content for a while to sit on the roof imbibing prodigious quantities of lemonade. Then his limbs began to twitch and his haunches to wriggle; and shortly afterwards he leaped to his feet and rushed to join the pullulating throng below.

'Greek, would you say?' said McPhee thoughtfully. 'Demeter? Persephone?'

'The Aalima? Oh, yes, definitely.'

McPhee looked pleased.

'Glad you think so, too. Cultic, I'm pretty sure.'

Owen would have liked to have gone down into the yard, not so much to dance – he regarded that as impossible – as to talk to some of the people there. At one point he did, indeed, descend the steps but the bottom of them was as far as he got. He stood there for a little while exchanging remarks with people he recognized.

Among those he recognized was Sayeed Abdullah, not dancing himself because of the decorum of age and his injured leg. He sidled round to Owen and greeted him shyly.

'Nice to see you here, Sayeed Abdullah.'

'Selim invited me. I said: You will have enough without me. But he said: No, no, the more the merrier. He is, indeed,' said Sayeed Abdullah gratefully, 'a most munificent person.'

'He is indeed.'

And as a result, thought Owen, would almost certainly be broke the following morning. The seniors in the Police Force, on Garvin's instructions, had tried to dissuade the constables and orderlies from too lavish expenditure on celebratory occasions. Births, naming days, circumcision feasts, weddings and funerals came round all the time and their cost was an important reason why the ordinary Egyptian was usually heavily in debt. The connection between the night before and the morning after was not very persuasive the night before, and the morning after, wise words were too late.

'Your wife is here, too, I gather.'

'Oh, yes, effendi, she is inside.'

Sayeed Abdullah drew near to Owen, looked over his shoulder and muttered: 'I've told her to stay near the baby and keep off the evil eye. It's the least we could do.'

'Oh, yes, very good idea. It's important to take care over such things.'

'Well, yes, effendi, especially as I've seen her do it before.'

Owen turned to him.

'Just a moment, Sayeed Abdullah; what was that?'

'I've seen her do it before, effendi. You remember, I mentioned it to you? The constable up from the country – the one who wouldn't pay his subscription?'

'I do remember. But, Sayeed Abdullah, what is it that you are saying? That the woman who cast the evil eye on that occasion was – the Aalima? Are you sure?'

'Yes, effendi. And that was why I was so worried. I did try and warn Selim, I could do no less after his kindness to me, but he said that you had bidden –'

'Let us be quite clear about this. The Aalima worked with Hassan? Perhaps still does work with Hassan?'

'I do not know about that, effendi, but I know that she did work with Hassan, that she came when he called. And what she did once –'

'Thank you, Sayeed Abdullah, that is most helpful.'

Owen went back up the steps and sat down again on his chair. Below him, in the yard, the music swirled and the men danced. Torches now were brought and fixed to the wall. In their fiery light he saw the excited, happy faces.

He went down the steps again and called to one of the women in the doorway.

'Is Aisha there?'

Shortly afterwards, Selim's wife appeared.

'Aisha,' said Owen, 'is the Aalima still with you?'

'She is, indeed, effendi. She feasts with us within.'

'I would like to see her,' said Owen. 'On the roof.'

Aisha went into the house and returned with the tall figure of the Aalima.

'Some questions about the ritual?' said McPhee, over Owen's shoulder.

'Some other questions first,' said Owen.

They drew back from the edge into the centre of the roof space, where it was quieter.

'There was a time,' said Owen, 'when you worked with a man named Hassan. He was an orderly at the police station. He worked for a Greek, Philipides effendi, and did his bidding. Among the things he did was collect money from the other orderlies and from new constables. If they refused to give, he would have them beaten; and sometimes he would do other things. Once, for instance, there was a man newly up from the country whose wife was having a baby, and he called a woman in and made her cast the evil eye. That woman was you.'

'What if it was?' said the Aalima.

'If it was,' said Owen, 'it was another thing to add to the many things that are piling up against your name. The heap will very soon topple over.'

'To cast the evil eye is nothing,' said the Aalima scornfully.

'To work against police officers is something,' said Owen. 'And to work with Hassan is something more.'

'Those are just words,' she muttered.

'They are more. You cannot go home tonight. You come with me to the Bab-el-Khalk.'

'I have done nothing!' she protested.

'You have worked with others who have done something. That is enough.'

For the first time she was shaken.

'If I have,' she said, 'it is very little.'

'That is perhaps so,' said Owen, 'and if it is, I will make a difference between you and the others. But only if you help me.'

'I have already told you everything —'

She stopped and looked at Owen.

'Tell me about Hassan.'

She shivered slightly and drew her shawl about her, even though beads of perspiration were running down her face.

'I had not seen him for some time,' she said, 'and then he came again.'

'When was this?'

'Before the Bimbashi came. He came to tell me the Bimbashi was coming. And what to do.'

'To put a drug in the drink?'

The Aalima inclined her head.

'And to arrange for him to be taken?'

'No, no,' said the Aalima, 'that was nothing to do with me. All I had to do was make sure the Bimbashi was drugged. Hassan would do the rest.'

'I shall ask him.'

She shrugged.

'He may say other,' she said, 'but I have told the truth.'

'All right,' said Owen, 'we will speak more tomorrow. Now we go to the Bab-el-Khalk.'

The Aalima followed him submissively. As they reached the steps, he turned to her.

'Perhaps I will speak with Hassan now,' he said. 'Where is he?'

'Effendi, I do not know. I never knew his house. He would always send when he wanted me.'

'But more recently he has come?'

'Yes, effendi, but I still do not know where he lives. He stays, I think, with his sister. It is in the Gamaliya somewhere.'

'What is the name of the sister?'

'I do not know. She is married. Her husband is, I think, a snake catcher.'

'That will do,' said Owen.

'It's *Al-Lewa* again, darling,' said Zeinab, folding up the newspaper. 'They're still after you, I'm afraid.'

'What is it now?'

'However, it's plainly false this time.'

'This time?'

'Well, the other time it was about women, and you know what you are –'

'Irreproachable,' said Owen, offended.

On any other occasion, Zeinab would have taken the matter up and developed, not to say embroidered, the theme. This morning, though, she was worried.

'It's about those stones,' she said. 'Both the diamond and the necklace. They know all about them and are asking what's happened to them. Darling –?'

'They're in a safe place,' Owen assured her.

'Not – not your pocket, by any chance?'

Owen pulled them out.

Zeinab came across.

'Look, darling, I don't normally question what you do, but I really do think this time – ! They are bound to ask what you are doing with them in your pockets.'

'I'm taking them round,' said Owen, 'to all the jewellers. And asking them who bought them.'

In Mahmoud's little office, with the three of them in there, the temperature was over 100. Sweat ran down Philipides's face in trickles; but that may, of course, have not been just due to the heat. He put his handkerchief to his forehead.

'It was done without my knowledge,' he said.

Mahmoud bent forward over his desk. He was less like a mongoose now than a bird of prey: one of the smaller hawks perhaps.

'Let us get this straight; when Hassan approached Police Officer Abdul Bakri and solicited money, it was with your knowledge; when he approached Orderly Sayeed Abdullah and solicited money, it was without your knowledge?'

'That is correct,' said Philipides, in a voice that was almost inaudible.

'Others were approached too. Can you tell me which of them were approached with your knowledge?'

'I cannot remember.'

'You remembered Abdul Bakri.'

'He was the one –'

'That Garvin found out about?' Mahmoud finished.

Philipides bowed his head.

'Which were the ones he did not find out about? Can you give me their names?'

'It is too long ago,' said Philipides wretchedly.

'Wasn't there a record?'

'Mustapha Mir –'

His voice died away. Mahmoud sat watching him.

'Mustapha Mir,' he said softly after a while. 'Tell me about him.'

Philipides made a weary gesture.

'What is there to tell? You know –'

'Have you spoken to him lately?'

'Spoken? How could I? He is in Damascus.'

'I thought you might have spoken when he gave you your instructions.'

'Instructions? What instructions?'

'You tell me.'

There was a little silence.

'I know nothing of any instructions,' said Philipides shakily.

Mahmoud gave him a moment or two. Then, without a sign being given, Owen knew it was his turn. The two had interrogated together before.

'Philipides,' said Owen softly, 'did you know that your wife had come to see me?'

'"Wife"?' said Philipides, eyes starting from his head. 'Wife?'

'Three times: once in an *appartement*, once in an arabeah, and once in my own house. She said it was without your knowledge. Is that true?'

'Wife? I haven't got a wife!'

'When she came to my house, she left a diamond behind. Deliberately. I wondered if that too, was without your knowledge?'

'I haven't got a wife,' said Philipides, moistening his lips.

'It is important, you see. Planting evidence, as, of course, you know, having been a police officer, is a crime. I was wondering if you wished to be charged with her.'

'I haven't got a wife,' said Philipides. 'I haven't got a wife! This is a trick!' he burst out. 'A plot! I haven't got a wife!'

'It will be easy to check,' said Mahmoud.

'Check, then!' said Philipides, turning on Mahmoud. 'Check!'

'She told me she was your wife,' said Owen.

'It is a lie! I haven't got a wife,' said Philipides, weeping.

Mahmoud looked at Owen. Owen knew that he was wondering if he had got it right. He was wondering himself.

'She said she was your wife.'

And then something came into his head, something that Selim had said as they walked away from the girl's *appartement*. Not Philipides's woman, but –

'Is it true that you are not married?' he said to Philipides.

'It is true! I swear! Check –'

'Perhaps it is true,' Owen said thoughtfully. 'But then, why –?'

He thought hard. Then –

'Philipides,' he said, almost gently, 'I really think that you should talk to Mr el Zaki. In your own interests. I think you may be right, that there *is* a plot against you. Only it is not I that am framing the plot, it is another, whom you know very well. Think for a moment: a woman comes to me and leaves a diamond. The diamond is later referred to in the press as evidence that I am guilty of accepting bribes. It is a plot against me. But at the same time, Philipides, it is a plot against you. For the woman claimed to be your wife. I can think of only one reason for that: she wished to incriminate you. Why was that, do you think?'

'I do not know. I have done nothing –'

'I will tell you. Because the man behind this wished to cover his tracks. At your expense. You know the man, I think. Perhaps you should tell Mr el Zaki about him.'

Paul brought the telegram to the club that evening and showed it to Owen. It was from Wainwright.

Suggest change venue Flower Show not time. Move closer to river. Heavy watering should do trick.

'Does that mean he's still coming?' said Paul crossly.

*   *   *

183

'Oh, my head!' gasped Selim. 'Oh, my head!'

'Just bloody get a move on!' snapped Owen.

'I come, effendi, I come! Oh, effendi,' said Selim, falling in beside Owen and clutching his head, 'do you think the Aalima put something in the drink again?'

'No, you just drank too much of it.'

Georgiades came up.

'I checked the names the teacher gave you,' he said. 'This was the only one who lived in the Gamaliya.'

'I want you to get them both,' said Owen. 'Both Hassan and the brother-in-law. Be careful with the brother-in-law. He may have a bag of snakes with him.'

'Snakes!' said Georgiades. 'What the hell do I do with them?'

'We ought to have brought a catcher, I suppose. Selim! The second man may have a bag with him. You take charge of that.'

'Abdul!' he heard Selim saying a little later. 'I'll take the man, you take the bag.'

'But, Selim —' pleaded Abdul's worried voice.

The house was part of a derelict block which backed on to waste ground.

'We'll have to cover the rear,' said Owen.

'You do that,' said Georgiades. 'I'll go in through the front.'

As they approached, a man detached himself from the shadow and came up to them.

'They're still there,' he said.

'Good,' said Georgiades. 'OK, we're putting somebody at the back, too. Take Owen effendi round and show him which house. I'll give you ten minutes,' he said to Owen.

There was a door at the back of the house and an outside staircase leading up on to the roof.

'Check if there's anyone up there,' whispered Owen. The man slipped silently away and returned in a moment shaking his head.

Owen put Selim one side of the door and Abdul the

other. Then he withdrew a little way with the third man so that they could deploy themselves as reserve.

It was the middle of the afternoon and there was no one about. Everyone was inside sleeping. The heat was intense. It felt as if a clothes iron was pressing between his shoulders. Sweat, merely from the walk, though in Selim's case probably also from the beer, was running down their faces.

Selim, listening at the door, suddenly held his hand up. Abdul twitched and raised his truncheon.

Then the door burst open and a man came running out.

Or would have come running out if Selim's great arms had not suddenly enfolded him.

'Not so fast, my lovely!' said Selim, and nodded his head to Abdul. Abdul struck once. Selim lowered his burden to the ground and sat on him.

As Owen came up, he caught the whiff of snake oil.

'Ah!' he said.

He stepped past and went on into the house. Somewhere a woman was screaming. He saw Georgiades in a doorway.

Georgiades nodded and stepped back. Owen followed him into the room. The only light came from one small window which had been part-blocked against the sun. There was a man lying on the floor. A constable knelt beside him forcing his arms up his back. As Owen came in, he turned his face towards him.

'Hassan?' said Owen.

13

The house was a fine old Mameluke house. To the street it presented a high wall, with a large wooden door, strong enough for a castle, in a richly decorated archway. There were no windows on the ground floor but above the archway a row of corbels allowed the first floor to project a couple of feet and above that were three rows of oriel windows closely screened with rich meshrebiya woodwork. The door opened into a courtyard along one side of which was the *mandar'ah*, or reception room, and it was there that Demerdash Pasha received him.

The *mandar'ah* had the usual sunken floor of black and white marble and in its centre one of the little fountains called *faskiya* played into a shallow pool lined with coloured marble. At one end of the room was a large dais with cushions, where the master of the house would welcome and entertain his guests if he felt so minded. Demerdash did not feel so minded and received Owen standing by the *faskiya*.

'I did not appreciate when we met, Pasha,' said Owen, after the formal greetings were over, 'that you were such a benefactor of the press.'

'Benefactor?'

'I gather that you are paying their fines. Or rather, *Al-Lewa*'s fines. Or so I understand.'

'What business is it of yours?'

'Oh, absolutely none. Except that I am the man who is imposing the fines. And I thought I would tell you the size of the sum you will be obliged to meet.'

He named the sum.

'But that is colossal!' cried Demerdash.

'Substantial, certainly. But then, so is the scale of the libel.'

'Outrageous!'

'You can test it in the Courts if you wish.'

'I certainly shall.'

'I am not sure that I would if I were you. You see, it would certainly emerge that the libels, in my case at least, were based on planted evidence.'

'You would have to prove that.'

'Oh, I could. I could even show where the stones had been purchased. And who had purchased them. And all that would come out at the subsequent trial.'

'Subsequent trial?'

'Well, naturally. These are serious charges that you would be faced with.'

'Why are you telling me this?'

'I thought you might prefer to restore your fortunes somewhere else. Damascus, let us say. You know Damascus, I think? It was there, wasn't it, that you met Mustapha Mir and enlisted his aid?'

'I don't know what you are talking about.'

'One of his friends, you see, has been telling me about the conversations you had with him. How you wished to do something that could restore the Khedive to his former powers. How he might be freed from the yoke of the British; and "the old virtues" – I quote – be restored.'

'Fantasy!'

'It was Mustapha Mir, I expect, who suggested how this might be done. Adroit as ever, he put forward a plan that coincided with his own interest. The three Englishmen who were primarily responsible for law and order would be discredited and obliged to leave. Men sympathetic to you, and the Khedive, would be put in their place. They might even include – or so, I think, Mustapha Mir hoped – a man who had held one of the posts before.'

'I know nothing of any such plan.'

'Not all the details, perhaps. They were left to Mustapha Mir. Mustapha Mir and some of his former employees. But you knew enough, in the article you planted in *Al-Lewa*, to refer to all three parts of the scheme: the drugging and exposure of McPhee, the accusations against Garvin and the charges against me.'

'What I have done,' said Demerdash, 'I have done for the sake of the Khedive.'

'No doubt. And now you are going to do him an even greater service. You are going to depart these shores for-ever. The arabeah is waiting at the door.'

'There wasn't a snowball's chance in hell,' he explained to Paul, 'of the Khedive agreeing to anything serious hap-pening to him. Besides, if we brought him to trial it would be an embarrassment to the Administration. All that stuff about McPhee –'

'All that stuff about you,' said Paul.

'Quite. And, of course, we didn't want him around making an even bigger nuisance of himself. So, all in all, it seemed best just to kick him out.'

Philipides, after a good scare, was left to moulder in peace. Hassan? Well, Mahmoud had got his teeth into him and didn't let go until he was well and truly sent down. He also made, in the interests of future efficiency, some Official Recommendations about recruitment and pro-motion in the Police Force. Rather to everyone's surprise, Garvin accepted them without hesitation. Indeed, it was rumoured that he and Mahmoud had had a joint hand in writing them.

The inquiry into Garvin's behaviour at the time of the Philipides business was quietly dropped.

'After all,' Paul pointed out, 'they'd done what they wanted: caused us political embarrassment.'

Wainwright did come out – he had left home, unfortu-nately, the very morning before the telegram arrived can-celling the request for him to give evidence – and was able to present prizes at the Flower Show. It was lucky that the hot spell had come to an end the week before in violent thunderstorms and heavy rain, thus obviating any need to change the Show's venue.

Owen, purely in the interests of cleaning everything up, or so he claimed, tried to lay his hands on – no, the wrong expression; better, apprehend – Mustapha Mir's woman but she had unfortunately just slipped out of the country. Owen did not mention all this to Zeinab.

Selim was seconded to the Mamur Zapt's staff, for special duties, which he found much more congenial than directing the traffic outside the Bab-el-Khalk. It carried with it an increase in rank to corporal, which put ideas into his head. His wife, Aisha, came to see Owen about some of them. Owen remonstrated with Selim.

'She's been a good wife to you,' he said. 'More to the point, she's brought you in some extra money. Would a new, more beautiful wife do that?'

'No, but she might do other things,' said Selim, ever hopeful.

The financial arguments proved in the end persuasive, especially as Owen hinted at the possibility of further employment for Aisha.

'After all,' said Selim, 'I can always get rid of one of the others.'

Commotion again in the Bab-el-Khalk. Sounds of doors banging, feet running. A mob of orderlies at Owen's door.

'Effendi, oh, effendi –' almost weeping. 'Come quick!'

Down into the courtyard.

'What is it?'

Pointing. The orderlies' lavatory again. And then, there, curled up in the very doorway, he could see it.

'Fetch the snake catcher!'

'Effendi, effendi!' Hands plucked at his arm. 'Not just there!'

But almost everywhere. In the patch of rough ground where every day McPhee tied up his donkey; in the bike shed where modernist Nassir effendi parked his new

189

bicycle; in the brickwork behind the tap in the yard – a crucial place, this, because it was where the orderlies went for drinking water; among the brooms and pails which the cleaners used every morning to scour out the Bab-el-Khalk; and out, lazily sunning themselves, on the very front steps of the police headquarters itself.

'Most interesting,' said McPhee, down there too. 'The plague of Egypt! Now what number was it?'

'What the hell have you done this time?' said Garvin, descending from his office.

'Effendi,' said Owen's own orderly, Yussuf, 'you really are in trouble. It's the Rifa'i. And Suleiman wants to use the –'

'Get Jalila.'

'Effendi, is this wise? You're in enough trouble as it is. That's what caused it in the first place.'

'Fetch her.'

'Effendi –' Then, seeing Owen was adamant, 'With her father?'

'Without her father.'

'Effendi – !'

But Jalila came. Even she blanched.

'You can do it, can't you?'

'Yes, but – effendi, you have been good to me, but in your own interest – the Rifa'i are strong. You will have to work with them.'

'I appoint you official snake catcher to the Bab-el-Khalk.'

'Yes, effendi, thank you, effendi. But –'

'What is it?'

'Effendi, it will be the same with all the buildings. I cannot do them all.'

The phone rang and Owen was summoned. It was Paul.

'Gareth, there's a slight spot of bother here at the Consulate-General –'

Owen returned to the courtyard.

'Could you do it if you had enough assistants?'

'Effendi, it is not wise. And I would not wish to. It would be to change too much.'

'She's right, Owen,' said McPhee.

'It was going to happen sometime,' said Jalila sadly. 'My father was wrong. I could never be a boy. I could never be one of the Rifa'i. Even you,' she said to Owen, 'cannot make me that. It is best to accept it. I will rid you of these snakes. But after that you must bring back the Rifa'i.'

Jalila set to work, watched by an enthralled crowd. At the end of the morning she placed two full, wriggling bags on the ground before Owen.

'I will pay you enough,' said Owen, 'for you to have a handsome dowry, so that you can marry the man of your choice. However, I would like to put another proposal to you, too. That is, that you should be on my payroll and work for me. I need more women among my agents.'

'Women on the payroll?' said Nikos faintly when he heard. 'This is worse than Cromer!'

Owen summoned the leaders of the Rifa'i.

'First, one of your members attacks the Bimbashi. Then there are snakes in the courtyard. It seems to me that there are but two ways for you to go. One is to the *caracol*, where you would stay for a long time; the other is that we should go back to the way things were.'

'Without the woman?' asked one of the Rifa'i leaders.

'Without the woman. Without an increase in pay, too.'

'It's a deal,' said the Rifa'i.

Printed by RR Donnelley at Glasgow, UK